I0726028

C.G. MACINGTON

Second Chapter

Rivera Publishing

First published by Rivera Publishing 2025

Copyright © 2025 by C.G. Macington

All rights reserved. No part of this publication may be reproduced, stored or transmitted in any form or by any means, electronic, mechanical, photocopying, recording, scanning, or otherwise without written permission from the publisher. It is illegal to copy this book, post it to a website, or distribute it by any other means without permission.

This novel is entirely a work of fiction. The names, characters and incidents portrayed in it are the work of the author's imagination. Any resemblance to actual persons, living or dead, events or localities is entirely coincidental.

C.G. Macington asserts the moral right to be identified as the author of this work.

First edition

Cover art by GetCovers

This book was professionally typeset on Reedsy.
Find out more at reedsy.com

Contents

I

Part One

Chapter 1

Thomas

The highway curves around the final bend, and Harbour Point unfolds before me like a forgotten photograph. The water glitters beneath the late summer afternoon sun, the same impossible blue I've described in a dozen fictional worlds but never quite captured.

My hands tighten around the steering wheel. Fifteen years since I left, swearing I'd never look back.

I slow as the "Welcome to Harbour Point" sign appears—freshly painted but the same weathered driftwood frame. Population four thousand nine hundred and eighty-two. Down three hundred from when I left. The familiarity hits like an undertow, pulling at something I've kept submerged for years.

"You're just here to write," I remind myself, voice hollow in the rental car's interior. Eight weeks to finish Captain Elian's fifth adventure or face my editor's wrath and my own failure. Eight weeks in the town I fled, where memories wait around every corner.

Main Street has changed, yet somehow hasn't. The hardware store where my father bought fishing tackle is now a boutique selling coastal-themed home goods. The diner remains, though its faded blue awning has been replaced with a sleek black one. New businesses with trendy logos occupy old storefronts, but the bones of the place—the narrow streets, the view of the Harbour, the salt-weathered charm—remain stubbornly intact.

I pass Whitman High School, and my throat tightens. The football field where I never belonged. The science lab where I excelled. The library with the hidden corner where Oliver and I...

My mind skitters away from the memory like a startled crab.

* * *

"You're really leaving?" Oliver's voice had cracked, his eyes fixed on the horizon rather than my face.

We sat on our beach, the hidden cove beneath the north cliffs where we'd spent countless afternoons and evenings. Where we'd first kissed twelve months earlier, terrified and exhilarated.

"Full scholarship to UCLA." The acceptance letter had arrived that morning, making real what had only been theoretical. "It's my chance, Ollie."

"I know." His fingers traced patterns in the sand between us, deliberately not touching mine. "I'm happy for you."

The lie hung between us, as tangible as the salt spray.

"You could apply for spring admission," I suggested, already knowing it was impossible. Oliver's father was sick. His family needed him here. The bookstore was struggling.

"Sure." Another lie.

I reached for his hand then, but he pulled away, standing abruptly. "We should get back before someone notices we're gone."

That night, alone in my bedroom, I made a promise to myself: I would never return to Harbour Point. This town was too small for what I wanted to become. Too small for what I felt for Oliver Chen.

* * *

The rental cottage appears exactly as advertised—a weathered blue clapboard perched on the bluff overlooking North Beach. My editor Vera found it, insisting isolation would help me focus. "No distractions, just you and your imagination," she'd said, not knowing she was sending me back to the one place guaranteed to distract me.

I park and sit motionless, watching waves crash against the shore below. From here, I can see the curve of the coastline, the jutting rocks that hide the small cove where Oliver and I escaped the town's watchful eyes. Our secret place.

My chest constricts. Is he still here? Married, probably. Kids, maybe. The thought brings a hollow ache with it that I've never fully extinguished.

The cottage key feels heavy in my palm as I finally exit the car. The realtor said someone would stock the kitchen basics. Six weeks of solitude stretches before me—just what I need to resurrect Captain Elian from the creative limbo where I've stranded her.

Inside, the cottage is all weathered wood and faded blue fabrics. Bookshelves line one wall, filled with well worn paperbacks left by previous occupants—beach reads and mysteries, their spines cracked from summer hands. The kitchen is small but updated, and beyond it, sliding glass doors open to a deck overlooking the water.

I drag my suitcase to the bedroom, unpack mechanically. Clothes in drawers. Toiletries in the bathroom. Laptop on the desk positioned to face the ocean view.

The last item in my bag is a framed review of my first novel, yellowed now. "Thomas Winters brings fresh energy to space opera with Captain Elian's debut adventure. His authentic emotional landscape elevates what could have been standard genre fare into something truly special and memorable."

I place it beside my laptop, then extract the folded newspaper clipping I keep inside my computer case—the review of the fourth and most recent book in the Captain Elian series. I smooth it flat, though I know the words by heart.

"Winters' latest Elian adventure delivers the normal expected action for the series but feels increasingly hollow and shallow, as if the author has lost connection to the emotional core that made his early work resonate with the reader."

Hollow. Shallow. The words haunt me. My editor calls weekly now, her voice tight with forced optimism. "How's the new manuscript coming, Thomas?" The answer is always the same: slowly. Painfully. Sometimes not at all.

I open my laptop and stare at the document titled "Elian5_draft." Thirty-eight pages of false starts and dead ends. My protagonist, once so vibrant in my mind, has become a stranger. The cursor blinks accusingly.

* * *

"What's this one about?" Oliver had asked, lying beside me on our beach, sand sticking to his bare shoulders. He held my notebook, reading the story I'd been too nervous to show anyone else.

"Just something stupid. A space explorer who finds these ancient ruins and—"

"It's not stupid." His eyes, serious behind his glasses, met mine. "You made me see it, Tommy. This planet that doesn't exist—I can see it."

Later, I'd name my protagonist's ship after him, a reference to the literal translation of Oliver's name. The Horizon, sleek and faithful, carrying Captain Elian through the stars. My readers never knew the significance, but with each book, I'd imagined him somewhere reading it, recognizing the tribute.

* * *

I close the laptop. Outside, the sun sinks toward the horizon, painting the water gold. The same view that inspired my first stories, the ones I scribbled in notebooks and only showed to Oliver.

Standing, I move to the sliding door and step onto the deck. The wind carries the scent of salt and pine, so familiar my body remembers it before my conscious mind can process the sensory input. I breathe deeply, letting Harbour Point fill my lungs again.

Below, the beach stretches empty in both directions. Tourist season hasn't started yet—another reason my agent thought this timing perfect. In the distance, I can just make out the rocks that hide our cove. Fifteen years, and I still think of it as "ours."

I wonder if the hollow feeling the reviewer identified began the moment I drove away from this town. From him. If Captain Elian's adventures grew emptier as I pushed the memories further down, denied the parts of myself I'd discovered here.

My phone vibrates in my pocket—my agent checking in. Again. The third time this week. I silence it without looking. Tomorrow I'll reassure her that the change of scenery is working, that words are flowing again. Another necessary lie to keep Vera and the publisher at bay while they await the manuscript that's now four months overdue.

The truth is, I've returned to Harbour Point carrying the same secret I left with: I am still in love with Oliver Chen, the boy I left behind. And I have no idea what I'll do if I see him again.

The sunset blazes fully now, the sky a canvas of orange and pink. In my novels, Captain Elian watches alien sunsets on distant worlds, always searching for something just beyond reach. I created her, but somehow never recognized we share the same restless hunger.

Maybe the critic was right. Maybe I've lost connection to something essential.

I return inside as darkness falls, the cottage suddenly too quiet. On the desk, my laptop waits, the unfinished fledgling manuscript a digital ghost. I open it again, scroll to where I abandoned my heroine in mid-adventure.

The cursor flashes. Once, twice, three times.

I begin to type.

Captain Elian stood at the viewport, watching the familiar planet grow larger. Fifteen years since she'd fled, promising never to return. But some orbits, once established, prove impossible to escape.

The words seem to come easier than they have in a long time. They're not good words, necessarily, but words nonetheless. I already know I'll likely delete them tomorrow, but for tonight, they're enough to break the silence.

Outside, waves crash against the shore of Harbour Point, the rhythm as familiar as my own heartbeat. I've come home, though I never meant to. Now I have to discover if anything remains of what I left behind.

Chapter 2

Thomas

I wake with a jolt, lifting my face off of the hard wood tabletop, to see the cursor still blinking on my screen. The words I wrote last night swim before my bleary eyes. Captain Elian returning home—subtle, Thomas. Real subtle.

Coffee. I need coffee.

After a quick shower, I pull on jeans and a button-down, then catch myself fussing with my hair in the mirror. Ridiculous. I'm just going into town for caffeine and maybe some groceries. Not to see anyone in particular.

The lie falls flat even in my own mind.

I know exactly where I'm going. Harbour Books. The thought of seeing Oliver again after all this time sends my heart racing like I'm twenty again. Pathetic. I'm a grown man, a published author, for Christ's sake. I've done book tours and television interviews. I've signed books for lines of people stretching out the door. I met Oprah.

So why does the thought of walking into one small-town bookstore terrify me?

I grab my keys and head out, the morning air crisp against my face. My generic rental car feels too conspicuous as I drive down Main Street, like everyone must know I'm back. The logical part of my brain knows this isn't true—most people wouldn't recognize me anyway—but anxiety rarely listens to logic.

When I reach Harbour Books, I drive past it twice before finding the courage to park. The storefront has changed. Gone is the faded blue paint and simple sign I remember. The building has been renovated with a modern glass facade, though the bones of the old Victorian structure remain. A new sign hangs above the door: "Harbour Books & Café" in elegant lettering. The display windows showcase colourful new releases and a chalkboard advertising today's coffee specials.

It's beautiful. Successful-looking. Nothing like the struggling rundown shop I remember from fifteen years ago when Oliver's father owned it and they struggled to make ends meet.

I sit in my car, hands gripping the steering wheel. This is stupid. I'm just going in for a book to get my creative juices flowing. Maybe a coffee. Completely normal.

I finally force myself out of the car and approach the entrance. Through the windows, I can see comfortable seating areas, customers browsing shelves. It's busy but not crowded. The perfect small-town bookstore atmosphere.

My hand hesitates on the door handle. What if he's not even here? What if he sold the place years ago? What if—

The door opens suddenly as a woman exits, nearly colliding with me.

"Sorry!" she says, stepping aside.

"My fault," I mumble, and before I can reconsider, I step inside.

A bell chimes softly overhead. The interior is even more impressive than the facade suggested—exposed brick walls, wooden shelves stretching to the ceiling, a small café area in one corner. The smell of books and coffee mingles in the air. Several customers browse quietly, a few seated in plush chairs with books open in their laps.

I drift toward the nearest shelf, pretending to browse while my eyes scan for Oliver. Maybe he's not working today. Maybe—

"I'll be right with you."

The voice comes from behind the counter, and though it's deeper than I remember, I'd know it anywhere. My stomach drops as a figure emerges from the back room, arms full of books.

Oliver.

He looks up, and the moment stretches between us. The books in his arms tilt dangerously as he freezes, recognition dawning on his face.

He's different—of course he is. His jet black hair now has a hint of threads of silver at the temples. He's filled out, no longer the lanky teenager I remember. He wears glasses with thicker frames than before, and a button-down shirt with the sleeves rolled up reveals forearms dusted with dark hair. He looks good, just how I imagined he would look when we were teenagers and deeply in love. A simple gold band gleams on his right hand—not his left, I notice immediately.

"Thomas?" His voice is quiet, controlled.

I manage a smile that feels stiff on my face. "Hi, Oliver."

He sets the books down carefully, methodically, buying time. I watch his hands—still elegant, still familiar despite the years between us.

"I didn't know you were in town." His tone is neutral. Professional.

"Just got in yesterday. I'm renting a place out on North Beach for a few months." I shove my hands in my pockets, unsure what to do with them. "Working on a new book."

He nods, maintaining the counter between us like a fortress wall. "That's... that's great."

A customer approaches with a question, and Oliver turns to her with visible relief etched across his face. I wander away, giving him space, pretending to be absorbed in the poetry section while my heart hammers in my chest.

The store is beautifully organized, with handwritten recommendation cards tucked into selected titles. I recognize Oliver's handwriting on some of them—still the same neat, precise script.

When I make my way around to the science fiction section, I stop short. It's not just any science fiction section—it's prominent, positioned near the front of the store, with an entire display dedicated to space exploration novels. And there, facing outward on the top shelf, all four of my Captain Elian books in a row. Even the collector's edition of the first novel with the alternative cover art.

My throat tightens. He's read them all. He must have.

"Find something interesting?"

I turn to see Oliver standing a few feet away, hands clasped tightly behind his back. The professional bookseller stance.

"Nice selection," I manage.

"Science fiction sells well." His tone is matter-of-fact. "Your books especially."

"I'm flattered."

An awkward silence stretches between us. There's so much I want to say, but none of it appropriate for this moment, this place, with customers browsing nearby.

"So," I gesture around, "you run Harbour Books now?"

He nods, something like pride briefly animating his features. "My dad passed ten years ago and left the place to me. We renovated five years back."

"It's beautiful. You've done an amazing job."

"Thank you." He adjusts his glasses, a gesture so familiar it aches. "It's been a labour of love."

Another customer calls for assistance, but Oliver ignores them for a moment.

"I should probably—"

"Of course," I say quickly. "Don't let me keep you."

He hesitates, then says, "We get a shipment of new releases on Thursdays if you're looking for something to read while you're in town."

"I'll keep that in mind."

He turns to go, then stops. "Actually, I should warn you—my daughter works here after school. She's a huge fan of Captain Elian. If she realizes who you are, she'll talk your ear off about space exploration."

The word "daughter" hits me like a physical blow. "Your daughter?"

"Lily. She's thirteen." His expression softens slightly. "Too smart for her own good and obsessed with your books."

"I'd be happy to meet her," I say automatically, mind still reeling. Daughter. Oliver has a daughter. Which means—

"You're married?" The question slips out before I can stop it.

Something shutters in his eyes. "Yes, her name was Sarah."

"Oh, I didn't know," I say, meaning it despite the shock still reverberating through me.

"No reason you would." His tone is gentle but final. He glances toward the customer still waiting. "I should get back to work."

"Right. Of course."

He nods politely and walks away, leaving me standing in front of my own books, feeling like I've been hit by a meteor. Oliver was married. Has a daughter. Built a life here while I've been—what? Chasing success? Running away?

My phone vibrates in my pocket, shattering the moment. I glance at the screen and my stomach sinks. Vera. Of course she'd call now.

"I need to take this," I mutter to no one in particular, already heading for the door.

The bell jingles as I step outside into the morning air, leaning against the brick exterior of Harbour Books.

"Vera, hi—"

"Thomas, darling, please tell me you've written something worth reading." Her voice cuts through pleasantries with surgical precision. "The publisher called me this morning, and I had to pretend I knew what was happening with your manuscript."

I run a hand through my hair, pacing a small circle on the sidewalk. "It's going well, actually. I've got a solid outline and the first three chapters are practically done."

The lie tastes bitter. I have exactly two paragraphs written, and they're terrible.

"I call bullshit." Vera doesn't miss a beat. "You've been saying the same thing for months. What's really happening?"

"I just needed a change of scenery. That's why I'm here. The words are coming now, I promise."

"Thomas." Her voice softens slightly. "You're not just my favourite client, you're my friend. But I need to be clear—this isn't a vacation. You're six months past your deadline. The publisher is talking about activating the breach clause in your contract."

My blood runs cold. "They wouldn't."

"They absolutely would. Four books is a complete series in their eyes. They'd happily slap 'The Complete Captain Elian Saga' on a box set and call it a day."

I close my eyes, leaning my head back against the brick. "I just need more time."

"You don't have more time. You have eight weeks. That's all I could negotiate. Eight weeks for a complete manuscript, fully edited, or they pull the plug. They're fed up with your stalling."

"Vera—"

"Eight weeks, Thomas. And I need something within two weeks to show them you're actually working on it and taking this seriously. Even a chapter. Something."

"Okay, you'll have it," I promise, knowing I'm digging myself deeper.

"Good. I'm always rooting for you, you know. Now go write and make me some money!" She hangs up before I can respond.

I stare at my phone, my reflection in the black screen looking pale and haunted. Eight weeks. Captain Elian deserves better than whatever rushed garbage I could produce in eight weeks.

The bell jingles again as I push back into the bookstore, searching for Oliver among the shelves. I need to finish our conversation, even if I'm not sure what to say next.

I select a random paperback from the shelf, needing something to do with my hands. Oliver helps the waiting customer, his manner professional and warm. I watch him from the corner of my eye, noting how he moves through the space he's created, confident and at ease.

When I approach the counter to pay, it's with the desperate hope he might suggest getting coffee, catching up properly. But he rings up my purchase efficiently, our fingers carefully avoiding contact when he hands me my change.

"Enjoy your stay in Harbour Point," he says, the same thing he probably says to every tourist.

"Thanks." I wait a beat too long. "The store really is wonderful, Oliver."

Something flickers in his eyes—pain? Regret? But it's gone before I can name it.

"Have a good day, Thomas."

The bell chimes as I exit, the sound cheerful and oblivious to the weight in my chest. Outside, I realize I don't even know what book I bought. I glance down at the cover—a romance novel. Of course.

I walk back to my car slowly, the invitation to catch up conspicuously absent. Not that I deserved one. What did I expect? That he'd welcome me with open arms after I left him behind? That he'd been waiting all these years?

He hasn't been waiting. He built a life—a beautiful one from the looks of it. A marriage. A child. A successful business. While I've been writing about fictional adventures, Oliver has been living a real life.

I sit in my car, staring at the storefront of Harbour Books & Café.

Through the window, I can see Oliver helping another customer, smiling in a way he hadn't smiled at me.

The hollow feeling expands inside me. I start the car and drive away, the romance novel sitting accusingly on the passenger seat beside me.

Chapter 3

Lily

I'm shelving the new shipment of fantasy novels when I overhear two women talking by the science fiction section. Their voices carry across the store even though they're trying to whisper.

"I swear it was him. Thomas Winters, in the flesh, buying coffee at The Daily Grind."

"No way. What would he be doing in Harbour Point?"

"Writing, probably. My cousin works at the rental agency and said someone famous took the North Beach cottage for the summer."

I freeze, a hardcover halfway to the shelf. Thomas Winters? The Thomas Winters? Author of the Captain Elian space adventures and basically the reason I survived middle school?

"I heard he's working on the fifth book," the first woman continues. "About time. It's been what, three years since the last one?"

"Four. And that ending! I need to know if Captain Elian survives the wormhole."

I slide the book into place and casually drift closer, pretending to straighten the nearby display.

"Did you talk to him?" the second woman asks.

"Are you kidding? I froze. Just stared like a bumbling idiot until he left."

Dad emerges from the stockroom with another box of books. He sets it down near me and gives my shoulder a gentle squeeze.

"Almost done, Lily? We can grab lunch after this shipment's shelved."

"Sure, Dad." I wait until he returns to the back before abandoning all pretense of work and moving directly to the women. "Excuse me, did you say Thomas Winters is in town?"

They exchange glances, and the taller one nods. "Saw him myself this morning."

"Do you know where he's staying?"

"Lily." Dad's stern voice comes from behind me, startling all three of us. "Let's not pester our customers."

The women assure him it's fine, but Dad gives me that look—the one that says we'll talk later—before returning to inventory.

"Sorry," I tell them. "I'm just a huge fan."

"North Beach cottages," the shorter woman whispers. "The blue one with the white trim."

I thank them and return to shelving, my mind racing with possibilities.

As soon as Dad disappears into his office for his afternoon accounting, I slip behind the checkout counter and grab my laptop. Thomas Winters in Harbour Point? This requires immediate investigation.

I pull up his official author website first. The "About" page has the basics—bestselling science fiction author, winner of the Nebula Award for his second Captain Elian novel, currently working on book five in the series. There's a professional photo of him looking constipated in a black turtleneck.

The tour schedule shows nothing for Harbour Point. In fact, there are no appearances scheduled at all for the next six months. Interesting.

I switch to social media and scroll through his sparse posts. Nothing about Harbour Point, but three days ago he posted a photo of a sunset over water with the caption: "New view, same stars. #writinglife"

Could that be our beach?

I dive deeper, searching "Thomas Winters Harbour Point" and click through several pages of results. A local newspaper article from fifteen years ago catches my eye: "Local Student Wins National Young Writers Award." The grainy photo shows a much younger Thomas accepting a trophy.

Wait. He's from here?

More searches lead me to his high school graduation announcement in the Harbour Point Gazette. Thomas Winters, valedictorian, heading to UCLA on a creative writing scholarship.

I lean back in the chair, processing this information. My favorite author grew up in my hometown, and now he's back. And Dad never mentioned knowing him, even though they must have been in high school around the same time.

Dad has always prominently displayed Thomas's novels in the bookstore. I assumed it was because they sell well, but now I wonder if there's more to it.

I check the time—3:15. Dad won't need me until closing at six. Plenty of time for a little expedition.

* * *

The walk to North Beach takes twenty minutes from downtown. I clutch my well-worn copy of "Captain Elian and the Rings of Persea" against my chest, its cover creased from countless readings. The book falls open naturally to my favourite passage, where Elian discovers the ancient star maps hidden within the rings.

The cottages appear ahead, a neat row of colourful buildings facing the water. The blue one with white trim sits at the far end, slightly separated from the others. A silver rental car is parked in the driveway.

My heart pounds as I approach the door. What if he's not home? What if he is home but doesn't want to be bothered? What if he's nothing like I imagined?

Too late to turn back now. I knock before I can change my mind.

Footsteps approach, and the door swings open. Thomas Winters stands before me, looking different from his author photo. He's taller than I expected, with dark-rimmed glasses and hair that's slightly dishevelled. He wears a faded t-shirt with "Whitman High Debate Team" printed across the front.

His eyebrows lift in surprise. "Hello?"

"Hi. I'm Lily." I thrust my book forward. "I'm sorry to bother you, but I heard you were in town, and I'm your biggest fan, and I was wondering if you might sign my book?"

The words tumble out in a rush. I take a deep breath and try again. "I'm Lily. I love your books."

His expression softens from confusion to amusement. "Well, Lily, it's nice to meet you. How did you find me?"

"Research. And eavesdropping, if I'm being honest."

He laughs—a genuine laugh that crinkles the corners of his eyes—and steps back from the doorway. "You'd better come in, then. Any fan dedicated enough to track me down deserves at least a signature."

The cottage interior is simple but cozy, with large windows overlooking the beach. What captures my attention, though, is the workspace set up in the corner—a laptop surrounded by stacks of notes, reference books, and hand-drawn star charts.

"You're working on book five," I excitedly blurt out.

He follows my gaze to the desk and sighs. "Trying to, anyway."

"Does Captain Elian escape the Cygnus Void? Because that ending was cruel, leaving readers hanging like that."

"You've read all four books?" He sounds genuinely surprised.

"Multiple times. I've also written three fan theories about how the quantum displacement might interact with the Persean technology to create a stable wormhole exit."

He stares at me for a long moment. "How old are you again?"

"Thirteen."

"And you understand quantum displacement theory?"

I shrug. "The basics. I've been reading about theoretical physics since I was ten."

He gestures to the couch. "Please, sit. I'd love to hear these theories."

I perch on the edge of the cushion, suddenly nervous now that he's taking me seriously. "Well, in book three, you established that Persean technology responds to thought patterns, right? And in book four, when Captain Elian entered the void, her consciousness began separating from her physical form."

Thomas sits across from me, nodding slowly.

"So my theory is that her fragmented consciousness could act as multiple anchor points across dimensions, creating a network that stabilizes the wormhole from collapse." I pause, watching his face. "Am I close?"

His mouth drops open slightly. "That's... remarkably insightful."

I can't help the grin that spreads across my face. "Really? Because I have more ideas about how the Ring Keepers might be involved."

"I'd love to hear them." He leans forward, genuinely interested. "But first, let me sign your book."

As he writes in my copy, I notice his handwriting—neat but with flourishes on certain letters. He hands it back with a smile.

"Thank you." I open to the inscription: "To Lily—the brightest star in the Harbour Point sky. Keep theorizing. —Thomas Winters"

"Now," he says, "tell me more about these Ring Keepers."

I launch into my theory, gesturing with my hands the way I do when excited. "The Ring Keepers were introduced as antagonists, but their motivation has always been preservation, not destruction. What if they recognized the danger of the void before anyone else? What if they've been trying to prevent catastrophic dimensional collapse all along?"

Thomas watches me with an intensity that would be unnerving if it weren't so validating. When I pause for breath, he says, "You remind me of someone."

"Who?"

He shakes his head slightly. "Just... someone I used to know. You have the same way of talking with your whole body when you're passionate about something."

I tilt my head, studying him. "You mean my dad?"

His expression freezes. "Your dad?"

"Oliver Chen. He owns Harbour Books."

Thomas sits very still. "Oliver is your father?"

"Yeah. Did you know him?"

"We went to high school together." His voice sounds careful, measured. "He mentioned he had a daughter when I saw him the other day at the bookstore."

"He doesn't talk much about the past." I trace the embossed lettering on my book cover. "Especially not since Mom died."

The room grows quiet. I didn't mean to mention Mom—it just slipped out.

"I'm sorry," Thomas says softly. "When did she pass?"

"Three years ago. Cancer." I don't elaborate. I've learned that adults get uncomfortable when I talk about Mom's death matter-of-factly, but that's just how I've learned to process it. "Dad took it hard. He tries to hide it, but I can tell."

Thomas nods, his eyes reflecting a sadness that seems deeper than just sympathy for a stranger. "Grief changes people."

"Did you know my mom too? Sarah Chen?"

"No, I... I left Harbour Point right after graduation. I didn't keep in touch with many people from here."

Something in his tone makes me wonder if there's more to the story, but I don't push. Instead, I redirect to safer territory.

"Can I ask about the Stellar Concordance? In book two, you mentioned seventeen member species, but you've only described twelve so far."

Thomas smiles, clearly relieved by the change of subject. "Very observant. The others will appear in future books."

"Including book five?"

He nods, leaning back in his chair. "You know, most readers don't catch those details."

"I make charts. And maps. I've been trying to recreate the Elian universe based on the star coordinates you include in the chapter headings."

His eyebrows rise. "You decoded those? They're actual astronomical coordinates."

"I know! That's how I figured out the Persean homeworld is in the Pleiades cluster."

Thomas laughs, shaking his head in amazement. "You're extraordinary, Lily Chen."

The way he says my full name makes me pause. There's something in his voice—a kind of wistfulness that doesn't make sense for someone who's just met me.

"How long will you be in Harbour Point?" I ask.

"The summer, at least. Until I finish this book."

I gather my courage. "Would it be okay if I came back sometime? I have more theories, and questions about the xenolinguistics in chapter seven of the third book."

He smiles, and it reaches his eyes. "I'd like that. But maybe check with your father first? I don't want him to worry about where you're going."

"Sure." I clutch my signed book to my chest. "Thank you for talking with me. Most adults don't take me seriously when I get into the serious science stuff."

"Their loss." He stands as I do. "It was a pleasure meeting you, Lily."

At the door, I turn back. "Mr. Winters?"

"Thomas, please."

"Thomas. The character of Captain Elian—she never gives up, even when everything seems impossible. That helped me a lot, after Mom died."

His expression softens. "I'm glad."

"I think..." I hesitate, then decide to be brave like Captain Elian. "I think Dad could use some of that never-give-up spirit too. He pretends he's fine, but he's lonely."

Thomas's face does something complicated—a mix of emotions I can't quite read. "Sometimes people need time to find their way back to themselves."

"Maybe. Or maybe they just need someone to show them the way." I smile. "See you around, Thomas."

As I walk away from the cottage, I can't help feeling like I've stumbled onto something important—a connection between my favourite author and my dad that neither of them has told me about. And if there's one thing I've learned from Captain Elian, it's that unexplored connections always lead to the most interesting discoveries.

Chapter 4

Thomas

I stare at the blank document on my laptop screen, the cursor accusingly blinking. Three hours, and I've written exactly seventeen words—all of which I've deleted and rewritten at least a dozen times.

"Captain Elian gazed at the twin moons of Altara Prime, knowing the galactic rebellion had begun."

It's not terrible. But it's not right either. Nothing about this book feels right. I push back from the desk and pace across the cottage's worn wooden floors. The windows frame a perfect view of the ocean, waves crashing against the shore in rhythmic certainty—unlike the chaotic mess inside my head.

I sit back down, fingers hovering over the keyboard. The words should come. They always have before. Four bestsellers, and now... nothing.

I type: "Oliver."

I stare at the name on the screen. Delete it. Type it again.

"Oliver Chen stands behind the counter of Harbour Books, his fingers tracing the spine of a novel he's read three times but still finds something new in."

The words flow suddenly, unexpectedly. This isn't Captain Elian exploring the outer reaches of the galaxy. This is something else entirely.

"His eyes—those deep brown eyes that seem to hold entire universes—scan the store with quiet pride. The reading nook in the corner where children gather for story time. The carefully curated staff picks display. The small café where locals linger over coffee and conversation. All of it bearing his imprint, his vision."

My fingers fly across the keyboard now, no hesitation.

"When he smiles—rare but worth waiting for—it transforms his face. The serious bookstore owner momentarily replaced by the boy who once pointed at constellations and dreamed of impossibilities. The boy who believed in me before I believed in myself."

I stop typing, my breath catching. This isn't my manuscript. This is... something else. Something dangerous. Something true.

I save the file without thinking, naming it "Oliver.docx" and close my laptop. The cottage suddenly feels too small, the walls closing in with memories I've done my best to keep locked away for fifteen years.

The first time I truly saw Oliver Chen, I was hiding.

* * *

It was a Friday night in October of my sophomore year. I'd discovered that Mr. Chen, the owner of Harbour Books, sometimes left the back door unlocked when he took out the evening trash. I'd never stolen anything—would never have considered it—but I'd discovered something far more valuable than merchandise: a safe place.

Home wasn't safe, not with my father's unpredictable moods and heavy hands. The school library closed at four, the town library at six. But Harbour Books had a science fiction section tucked into the back corner, partially hidden by a tall bookshelf, with a worn armchair that nobody seemed to use.

I'd slip in after closing, find my hidden corner, and read by the dim security light until Mr. Chen arrived to open the next morning. Then I'd pretend I'd just come in early, buy a cheap paperback with whatever money I'd managed to scrimp and save, and leave before he could start asking questions.

That particular Friday, I'd brought my notebook. I wasn't just reading science fiction anymore—I was writing it. Terrible, derivative stories about space explorers and alien worlds, but they were mine. My escape from reality.

I didn't hear him approach. One moment I was alone in my corner, scribbling furiously about Captain Elian's first encounter with the crystalline beings of Proxima Centauri, and the next—

"We're closed."

I jumped, my notebook falling to the floor. Standing before me was a boy about my age, with dark hair that fell across his forehead and serious eyes behind wire-rimmed glasses.

"I—I'm sorry," I stammered, scrambling to gather my things. "I didn't—I'll go—"

"You're Thomas Winters." Not a question. "We have English together. Mrs. Patterson's class."

I paused, finally looking at him properly. Oliver Chen. Quiet, smart Oliver who sat two rows ahead of me, who always had the right answer but never volunteered it unless called upon.

"Yeah," I managed. "You're Oliver."

He nodded, then glanced at my fallen notebook, pages splayed open. Before I could stop him, he bent down and picked it up, eyes scanning the page.

My face burned with shame. No one had ever read my stories. No one.

"Is this yours?" he asked, still looking at the page.

I nodded, unable to speak, waiting for the mockery. The laughter. The inevitable judgment.

"This is good," he said quietly.

I blinked, certain I'd misheard. "What?"

"This description of the crystalline beings. How they refract light differently based on their emotions." He looked up at me, those serious eyes suddenly alive with interest. "I've never thought about aliens communicating that way before."

The tension in my shoulders eased slightly. "You... like science fiction?"

A small smile—the first I'd ever seen from him. "My dad owns a bookstore. I like everything, even the romance dad says I'm too young to read."

He handed the notebook back to me, then glanced around as if suddenly remembering where we were. "How did you get in here? We closed two hours ago."

The shame returned, hot and heavy in my chest. "The back door was unlocked. I'm sorry. I wasn't stealing anything, I swear. I just... needed somewhere to go."

Something in his expression shifted, understanding replacing suspicion. "You come here a lot after hours, don't you? Dad thought he was going crazy, finding books moved around in the morning."

I looked at the floor. "I always put them back exactly where I found them."

"Except for that copy of Dune that ended up in the Romance section last month."

I winced. "That was an accident. It was dark."

To my surprise, Oliver laughed. Not mockingly—a genuine laugh that transformed his serious face into something beautiful. "Come on," he said, gesturing for me to follow him.

I hesitated, clutching my notebook to my chest. "Am I in trouble?"

He shook his head. "No. But if you're going to keep breaking in, you should at least have better light to read by."

I followed him through the darkened store, past shelves of books that loomed like friendly giants in the dim light. He led me to a door marked "Staff Only" and opened it, revealing a small room with a desk, a mini-fridge, and a comfortable-looking couch beneath a window.

"Dad's office," Oliver explained. "He won't be back until morning. You can stay here if you want. The light's better, and there's sodas in the fridge."

I stood frozen in the doorway, unable to comprehend this unexpected kindness. "Why would you... I mean, you don't even know me."

Oliver shrugged, suddenly looking embarrassed. "I know what it's like to need a safe place." He gestured to my notebook. "And I want to know what happens next. With the crystalline beings."

Something warm unfurled in my chest, something I didn't have a name for yet. "You really want to read my story?"

He nodded, that small smile returning. "Only if you want to share it."

I hesitated only briefly before handing him the notebook. "It's not finished."

"The best stories never really are," he said, settling onto the couch and opening to the first page.

I stood awkwardly for a moment before joining him, leaving careful space between us. As he read, I watched his face, the way his expressions changed, the small nods of appreciation, the raised eyebrows at plot twists. No one had ever looked at my words that way before.

When he finished the available pages, he looked up at me with those serious, wonderful eyes. "You're really good. Like, really good."

"You're just being nice."

He shook his head firmly. "I read everything, remember? I know good writing when I see it." He handed the notebook back. "You should finish it."

"I will," I promised. "I have ideas for where it goes next."

Oliver leaned back against the couch cushions, looking at me with curiosity. "How did you get interested in space stuff?"

I shrugged. "I've always liked looking at the stars. They make me feel..." I trailed off, embarrassed to admit the truth.

"Less alone?" he suggested quietly.

I looked at him, startled by his perception. "Yeah. Exactly. Like, there's so much out there, so many possibilities. It can't all be... like here."

"What's wrong with here?" he asked, but his tone suggested he already knew the answer.

I stared at my hands. "My dad drinks. A lot. And when he drinks, he gets... mean."

Oliver was quiet for a moment. "My mom left when I was eight. Just... disappeared. Dad doesn't talk about it, but I think she couldn't handle having a family. Having me."

The confession hung between us, a shared vulnerability that felt both terrifying and exhilarating.

"That's why I like the stars too," Oliver continued, moving to the window and looking up at the night sky. "All those possibilities. All those other worlds where things might be different."

I joined him at the window, our shoulders almost touching. "Do you ever wish you could just... go? Leave everything behind and start over somewhere else?"

"All the time," he admitted. "But then I think about my dad, working so hard to keep this place going, to give me a good life. And I think maybe... maybe this is where I'm supposed to be. For now."

I looked at his profile, illuminated by moonlight streaming through the window. The straight nose, the serious mouth that occasionally yielded the most wonderful smile, the eyes that seemed to see right through me.

"Maybe some people are like stars," I said without thinking. "They're exactly where they're supposed to be, creating constellations with the people around them."

Oliver turned to me, our faces suddenly close. "And what about you, Thomas Winters? Are you where you're supposed to be?"

In that moment, standing in the back office of Harbour Books with this boy I barely knew but somehow understood me, I felt something click into place. A recognition. A possibility.

"Right now?" I whispered. "Yeah. I think I am."

His smile then—shy but real—outshone every star in the sky.

* * *

The memory fades, leaving me standing at the cottage window, staring at the same stars we once named together. Fifteen years later, and I can still feel the electricity of that first real conversation, the moment when my lonely universe suddenly expanded to include another person.

I return to my laptop and open the document I'd started. "Oliver.docx" glows on the screen, a digital confession of feelings I've never fully put into words.

My editor wants the next Captain Elian adventure. The fans are waiting for their hero to continue exploring the galaxy.

But the story that's burning to be told isn't about distant planets or alien civilizations. It's about a boy who found another boy hiding in a bookstore after hours. About stars and possibilities. About roads not taken and words left unsaid.

I begin to type again, the words flowing like they haven't in months. Not my contracted manuscript, not the story I'm supposed to be writing.

But maybe—just maybe—the story I need to tell.

* * *

Oliver

The house settles into silence after Lily goes to bed. Her footsteps pad down the hallway, followed by the click of her bedroom door. I listen for a moment longer, making sure she's actually turning in rather than sneaking onto her e-reader to read under the covers.

No light spills from beneath her door. Good. She needs her sleep.

I pour myself a finger of whisky—the bottle Sarah's brother gave me last Christmas that I rarely touch—and wander into my study. The small room tucked behind the kitchen holds most of my personal books, the ones I don't keep downstairs in the store. A half-moon spills silver light through the window, illuminating the shelves that line three walls from floor to ceiling.

The whisky burns pleasantly as I sink into my leather chair, the one indulgence I allowed myself after Sarah died. It still smells new despite three years of me sitting here, often just staring at the wall, trying to figure out what comes next. For me. For Lily.

My eyes drift to the bottom shelf of the bookcase directly across from me. The cardboard box has sat untouched for years, pushed far back against the wall. I've never had the courage to look through it, not really. Not properly.

But tonight feels different. Maybe it's because Thomas is back in town. Maybe it's because Lily came home bubbling with excitement about meeting her favourite author, completely unaware of who he once was to me.

"He knew you in high school, Dad!" she'd said, eyes wide with wonder. "Why didn't you ever tell me you went to school with Thomas Winters?"

I'd shrugged, kept my voice neutral. "We weren't close."

The lie had tasted bitter on my tongue.

I set my glass down and cross to the shelf, kneeling to pull the box forward. A thin layer of dust coats the top, and I brush it away before lifting the lid.

Inside are the pieces of a life I'd packed away. Graduation tassel. A few photos from high school. The small shell collection from the hidden cove. And beneath it all, a manila folder tied with a faded blue ribbon.

My hands shake slightly as I untie it.

The folder contains clippings—literary magazines, small press publications, a few printouts from online journals. All containing Thomas's early work, before the novels, before Captain Elian became a household name among science fiction readers.

I flip through them chronologically, watching his writing evolve from clumsy teenage metaphors to the confident voice that would eventually capture thousands of readers. I remember how he used to read his stories to me, how his face would light up when I responded to a particular line or character.

Near the bottom of the stack, I find it. The first real publication, in a literary magazine that had seemed so prestigious at the time. "Distant Lights" by Thomas Winters. A short story about a boy who builds a telescope to watch for aliens but instead discovers the constellations of human connection in his own backyard.

I run my fingers over the printed page, remembering how he'd burst into the bookstore waving the acceptance letter, how we'd celebrated behind the astronomy section with kisses that tasted of possibility.

When my copy arrived in the mail, he'd already inscribed it. I turn to the title page now, and there it is, just as I remember:

For O—who taught me to see the stars even on cloudy nights.

And beside the inscription, drawn in blue ink that has faded slightly over the years: the constellation Orion. My constellation, he'd called it. Strong and steady in the winter sky.

"Damn it, Thomas," I whisper to the empty room.

I flip the magazine closed and press it against my chest for a moment, allowing myself to remember. The way his hand felt in mine. The sound of his laugh echoing in the empty bookstore after hours. The plans we'd made, whispered between kisses in that hidden cove where no one could find us.

Plans that fell apart when he left for college and I stayed behind, too afraid to follow, too afraid to be who I really was.

I reach for my whisky and drain it in one swallow.

After Thomas left, I'd made my choices. Pushed down those feelings. Met Sarah in the nearby community college. Built a life that made sense to everyone, including my traditional Chinese father who never would have understood a son who loved another boy.

Sarah had been kind, beautiful, smart. I'd loved her—not with the consuming fire I'd felt for Thomas, but with a steady warmth that grew over time. She gave me Lily, the greatest gift of my life. I never regretted marrying her, even if late at night, I longed for roads not taken.

When she got sick, everything else fell away. Nothing mattered except taking care of her, then taking care of Lily after she was gone. I haven't had time to think about who I am, what I want. Haven't allowed myself that luxury.

But now Thomas is back, and the feelings I've kept buried are surfacing like air bubbles in water.

I pull out my phone and find myself scrolling to his contact information. The bookstore keeps records for author events, and I'd added his number to my phone just yesterday, telling myself it was purely professional.

My thumb hovers over his name. What would I even say? *Hey, remember when we were seventeen and head over heels in love but I was too scared to choose you?*

I toss the phone onto the desk and turn back to the box. Beneath the folder of Thomas's stories, I find a stack of photographs. Most are from high school—drama club performances, debate team competitions, graduation.

And then I find one I'd forgotten about. Thomas and me at the beach, sitting close together on a blanket, our shoulders touching. His head is turned toward me, caught mid-laugh, while I'm looking at the camera with a small smile. Anyone who saw it would think we were just friends, but I remember the moment. How his hand was covering mine just out of frame. How my heart felt too big for my chest.

We were so young. So full of possibility.

I flip the photo over. On the back, in Thomas's messy handwriting: *O & T, North Beach, July 2009.*

Two months before he left for college. One month before everything fell apart.

I set the photo aside and continue digging. At the very bottom of the box, I find a small, worn notebook. Thomas's notebook, the one he carried everywhere senior year, scribbling ideas for stories. He must have left it behind, or maybe given it to me. I can't remember now.

I open it carefully, the binding cracked with age. Inside are fragments of stories, character sketches, bits of dialogue. And scattered throughout, little notes addressed to me.

O—what if Captain Elian discovers a planet where time moves backward?

O—do you think this character name works?

O—I love you. In case I haven't said it enough today.

My chest tightens. I close the notebook and put it back in the box, along with everything else except the published story. That, I set aside on my desk.

I pour another finger of whisky and carry it to the window. The night is clear, stars scattered across the sky like diamonds on black velvet. Somewhere across town, Thomas is looking at these same stars. Maybe even thinking of me.

My phone sits on the desk, silent and accusing.

I should call him. Clear the air. At the very least, thank him for being kind to Lily today.

But what would come after that? Awkward reminiscing? Painful acknowledgement of what we lost? Or worse—what if the connection is still there, humming between us like a live wire? What then?

I have Lily to think about. The bookstore. The life I've built here.

Thomas is only in town temporarily, working on his book. Then he'll leave again, back to his real life in New York or wherever successful authors live these days. And I'll still be here, picking up the pieces of whatever this brief re-connection breaks loose in me.

No. Better to keep things as they are. Professional. Distant. Safe.

I down the rest of my whisky and set the glass in the sink on my way to my bedroom. As I pass Lily's room, I pause, listening to her soft, even breathing. She deserves stability. Certainty. Not a father suddenly questioning everything about himself because his high school sweetheart showed up after fifteen years.

In my bedroom, I change for sleep and slide under the covers, but rest doesn't come. Instead, I stare at the ceiling, thinking about Thomas's face when he walked into the bookstore yesterday. The flash of recognition, of pain, of something else I couldn't name. The careful way he'd asked about my life, as if testing the boundaries of what was safe to discuss.

My phone buzzes on the nightstand—a text message. I reach for it, squinting at the sudden brightness of the screen.

It's from Lily: *Forgot to say goodnight. Love you, Dad.*

I smile in the darkness. *Love you too. Now go to sleep.*

Three dots appear, then: *Mr. Winters invited me to visit again tomorrow. He's going to show me how he plans his books. Is that okay?*

My thumb hovers over the keyboard. I should tell her no. Create distance. Protect us both from whatever complicated emotions Thomas's presence stirs up.

But Lily loves his books. She's been talking about Captain Elian for years. And Thomas was kind enough to entertain her questions today.

That's fine. Be home for dinner.

Thanks Dad! Goodnight for real this time.

I set the phone down and close my eyes, but sleep remains elusive. In the darkness, I see Thomas's face as it was at seventeen—bright with ambition and love—overlaid with the man who walked into my bookstore yesterday, carrying the weight of fifteen years between us.

I won't call him. I won't seek him out. But I can't stop Lily from visiting, from forming her own connection to the author she admires.

And if that means our paths cross again... well, I'll just have to remember that the past is past, and some stars burn too brightly to orbit for long.

Chapter 5

Oliver

I watch Lily push her broccoli around her plate, barely containing her excitement. She's been like this since she got home—vibrating with energy, her words tumbling out so fast I can hardly keep up.

"And then Mr. Winters showed me his storyboard for the whole series! He has these character sheets with details that never even made it into the books." She stabs a piece of chicken. "Did you know Captain Elian has a scar on her shoulder from when she was ten and fell out of a tree on her home planet? It's never mentioned in the books, but Mr. Winters says it affects how she carries himself."

"That's interesting," I say, trying to sound appropriately impressed while keeping my emotions in check. It's strange hearing Thomas's name spoken so casually in my home, like he belongs here. "You seem to have had a good time."

"The best! He answered all my questions about the Varian Nebula and why the physics works the way it does in his universe." She takes a quick bite, chews hurriedly. "And guess what? The spaceship—the Horizon—it's named after someone real!"

My fork freezes halfway to my mouth. "Is that so?"

"Yeah! He wouldn't tell me who, though. Said it was personal." She narrows her eyes at me. "Dad, you went to school with him, right? Do you know who it's named after?"

I set my fork down carefully. "Thomas and I weren't close friends, Lily. Just classmates."

The lie tastes bitter. I take a sip of water to wash it away.

"Well, anyway, he showed me his writing process. He has this whole ritual where he makes tea and lights this special candle and puts on instrumental music." She leans forward. "But he's stuck on this book. Really stuck. He says it's not working the way the others did."

"Writing can be difficult," I offer neutrally, though my mind races with memories of Thomas hunched over notebooks, scribbling furiously, then reading passages aloud to me under starlight.

"I had an idea," Lily says, her voice taking on that tone she uses when she's about to suggest something she thinks I might resist. "What if we hosted an author event at the store? For Mr. Winters?"

I blink at her. "An author event?"

"Yeah! We could advertise it in the paper and on social media. I bet people would come from all over the coast to meet him." Her eyes light up. "We could sell his books—I checked, and we only have three copies left of *Beyond the Varian Nebula*—and maybe do a reading and Q&A."

"Lily..."

"It would be great for business, Dad." She's using her reasonable voice now. "You're always saying we need to attract new customers to compete with the online stores. This would bring people in who might never have visited otherwise."

She's not wrong. Author events are good for business. We hosted Madeline Chen last year—no relation, despite sharing a last name—and sold more cookbooks in one day than we had in the previous six months.

But Thomas isn't Madeline Chen. Thomas is...complicated.

"I'll think about it," I say, buying time.

"Dad." Lily gives me her most serious look. "Mr. Winters is famous. Like, really famous. And he's right here in Harbour Point! It would be weird if our bookstore didn't host an event."

I sigh. She's right again. It would look strange if we ignored the presence of a bestselling author in our small town, especially one with local roots.

"Besides," she adds, her voice softening, "I think he's lonely."

"Lonely?" I look up sharply.

She nods. "He has this big empty cottage and he's just there by himself, writing. Or trying to. No visitors except me." She pushes her plate away. "I think he could use some friends."

The thought of Thomas alone in that cottage by the beach, struggling with his writing, creates an ache in my chest I don't want to examine too closely.

"Fine," I concede. "I'll call him after dinner and see if he's interested."

Lily's face lights up like I've just given her the best gift imaginable. "Really? You will?"

"Yes, but I'm not promising anything. He might be too busy, or not interested in doing public events."

"He'll say yes," she says with her usual complete confidence. "I know he will."

After dinner, Lily helps clear the table, humming to herself. I watch her move around the kitchen with an ease that reminds me of Sarah. The same efficient movements, the same little smile when she's pleased with herself.

Sarah would know what to do about Thomas. She always had a knack for navigating complicated situations with grace. But Sarah isn't here, and I'm left making these decisions alone.

Later, after Lily's gone to bed, I sit at my desk with my phone in hand. Thomas's number is written on a scrap of paper—Lily gave it to me "just in case." My finger hovers over the keypad.

This is ridiculous. I'm a grown man, a business owner. I can make a simple professional call to a local author about an event that would benefit my store. There's nothing personal about it.

Except everything with Thomas has always been personal.

I dial before I can talk myself out of it. The phone rings once, twice, three times. I'm about to hang up when he answers.

"Hello?" His voice is deeper than I remember, rough around the edges. Like he hasn't used it much today.

"Thomas? It's...it's Oliver. Chen." I wince at my awkwardness.

A pause. "Oliver." He says my name like he's testing the weight of it. "Is everything okay? Is Lily alright?"

"Yes, she's fine. She's great, actually." I clear my throat. "She had a good time with you today. Thank you for being so generous with your time."

"She's a remarkable kid. Smart as a whip. You must be very proud."

"I am." I stare at the photo of Lily on my desk, taken last summer at the beach. "Listen, I'm calling because—well, Lily had an idea. About the bookstore."

"Oh?"

"We host author events sometimes. Readings, signings, that sort of thing. And since you're in town..." I trail off, suddenly uncertain.

"You want me to do an author event at Harbour Books?" Thomas sounds surprised, but not displeased.

"If you're interested. No pressure. I know you're here to work on your book, and I don't want to impose—"

"I'd love to," he cuts in. "Really, Oliver. It would be my pleasure."

I blink, caught off guard by his easy acceptance. "Great. That's...great. We could do it next week, maybe? Give us time to advertise?"

"Next week works for me. Whatever day is best for you."

"Thursday evening? Around seven?"

"Thursday at seven it is." There's a smile in his voice now. "It'll be nice to see the store in action again."

"Thank you." I fidget with a pen on my desk.

A beat of silence stretches between us, laden with unspoken words.

"Oliver," Thomas says finally, his voice softer. "I know this is probably awkward for you. Having me back in town, spending time with Lily. If you're uncomfortable with any of it—"

"It's fine," I interrupt, not ready to have this conversation. "Really. Lily enjoys your company, and the event will be good for the store."

"Okay." He doesn't sound entirely convinced. "But if that changes—"

"It won't." I take a deep breath. "So, Thursday at seven. We usually do a reading, then a Q&A, followed by the signing. Does that work for you?"

"Perfect." Another pause. "It'll be good to see you, Oliver. Properly, I mean. Not just a quick hello in the store."

My heart does something complicated in my chest. "Yes, well. I should probably go over some details with you before the event. Maybe you could come by the store earlier on Thursday? We close at five before evening events to set up."

"I'll be there at five," he says. "Goodnight, Oliver."

"Goodnight, Thomas."

I hang up and set the phone down carefully, as if it might explode. What am I doing? Inviting Thomas into my space, creating an opportunity to be alone with him. It's asking for trouble.

But it's just business, I tell myself. A professional courtesy. Nothing more.

* * *

Thomas

The line goes dead. I stare at my phone, the screen dimming, then turning black. The silence in my rental cottage suddenly feels oppressive.

"What the hell did I just agree to?" I mutter to the empty room.

I drop the phone onto the couch and pace across the hardwood floor, running my fingers through my hair. The reality of what I've just committed to crashes over me like a wave. In two days, I'll be standing in Harbour Books—Oliver's space—surrounded by people expecting me to be Thomas Winters, celebrated author. Meanwhile, I'll be fighting to keep my eyes off the one person in the room who knows I'm just Tommy, the boy who used to hide among his shelves.

My heart hammers against my ribs. I haven't done a reading in over a year, not since book four came out. My publisher stopped pushing for appearances when it became clear I was struggling with the next instalment. And now I've agreed to do one in the most emotionally complicated venue possible.

"Shit, shit, shit."

I grab my laptop and open a new document, trying to outline what I'll read. Nothing from the current manuscript—it's too raw, too real, too much about the man who'll be standing five feet away from me. Maybe something from book three? The rescue mission to Proxima Centauri was always a crowd-pleaser.

My fingers hover over the keys, but instead of typing notes for the reading, I find myself searching through old files. I scroll past drafts and outlines until I find a folder simply labeled "HC" – Harbour Cove. I hesitate before clicking it open.

Inside are dozens of documents dating back to my freshman year of college. Journal entries. Abandoned letters. Fragments of stories where the protagonist always somehow resembled a quiet, thoughtful Chinese-American boy with careful hands and eyes that crinkled when he laughed.

I click on one dated August 17, fifteen years ago. The night before I left for college. The last time Oliver and I were truly alone together.

***

The moon hangs low over the water, casting a silver path across the dark surface. It's almost midnight, and the hidden cove feels like it exists outside of time—our private universe.

Oliver sits beside me on the blanket we've spread across the sand, our shoulders touching. We haven't spoken in several minutes. What is there to say? Tomorrow I leave for Berkeley, five thousand kilometres away. He stays here to help his father run the bookstore.

"I could defer," I say suddenly, breaking the silence. "Take a gap year."

Oliver turns to me, moonlight catching in his dark eyes. "No, you can't."

"Why not? Plenty of people take gap years."

"Because you'd resent me for it." His voice is soft but certain. "Maybe not right away, but eventually."

I want to argue, but the truth of his words stings. I've dreamed of Berkeley since sophomore year, of studying creative writing there, of finally escaping the suffocating smallness of Harbour Point.

"We could try long distance," I suggest, though we've had this conversation before.

Oliver looks out at the water. "Tommy... you know why we can't."

I do know. His father doesn't know he's gay. No one does except me. Oliver isn't ready to come out, not in this town, not with his traditional family expectations. A long-distance relationship would mean phone calls he couldn't take at home, explanations for why he's saving money for plane tickets, lies upon lies upon lies.

"I'll come back for you," I say, the words bursting from some desperate place inside me. "After college. Four years. I'll come back and—"

"Don't." He cuts me off, his voice breaking. "Don't make promises we both know you can't keep."

I turn his face toward mine, needing him to see my sincerity. "I mean it, Ollie. Four years. I'll be back."

His eyes shine with unshed tears. "You're meant for bigger things than this town, Tommy. We both know that."

I kiss him then, pouring everything I can't say into it. His hands come up to frame my face, thumbs brushing over my cheekbones. When we finally break apart, both breathing hard, I rest my forehead against his.

"I love you," I whisper. It's the first time I've said it out loud.

Oliver's eyes close, pain flashing across his features. "I love you too," he whispers back. "That's why I can't ask you to come back."

* * *

I slam the laptop closed, my breath coming too fast. Fifteen years, and the memory still cuts like glass.

I didn't go back after four years. By then, I'd sold my first novel and was deep into writing the second. Book tours, conventions, a life I'd only dreamed of was suddenly mine. And Oliver... according to Lily, he married a woman named Sarah about fourteen years ago.

"Fuck," I mutter, pushing away from the desk.

I need air. Grabbing a light jacket, I step outside onto the porch of the rental cottage. The night is clear, stars scattered across the sky like spilled salt. Down below, I can just make out the curve of the shoreline, the hidden cove invisible from this angle but present in my mind.

How am I supposed to stand in front of a crowd in Oliver's bookstore and pretend we're just old classmates? How do I read from books that, in so many ways, were written for him?

Captain Elian, my protagonist, was always part Oliver—thoughtful, principled, carrying the weight of responsibility on her shoulders. The spaceship *The Horizon* was named for what Oliver once told me about his name: "Chen means dawn or daybreak in Chinese—the horizon where the sun rises." I wove pieces of him into every page, and now I have to pretend it was all just imagination.

I pull out my phone and scroll to my agent's number. One call and I could cancel. Claim writer's block, illness, anything. But my thumb hovers over the screen without pressing call.

Cancelling would mean running away again. It would mean letting Oliver believe I came back to Harbour Point without any thought of him, that I could be in the same town and not want to see him. It would mean denying myself even this small connection to the person who first believed in my stories.

I pocket my phone and go back inside. If I'm going to do this, I need to prepare. Not just the reading itself, but emotionally. I need armour.

At my desk, I pull out a fresh notebook and begin to write. Not fiction this time, but boundaries. Rules for myself:

- Keep conversation professional
- Don't mention the past unless he does
- No lingering looks
- Don't ask about his marriage
- Remember he has a life here—one that doesn't include you

I stare at the list, then add one more item:

- Remember why you really came back to Harbour Point

The truth is, I didn't choose this town randomly to finish my book.

I didn't pick it because the advance praise for the rental cottage mentioned the perfect writing desk overlooking the ocean. I came back because I'm stuck—not just in my writing, but in my life.

Something is missing from the story I'm trying to tell, and I've known for a while what it is. Captain Elian has explored the furthest reaches of the galaxy, faced down alien civilizations and cosmic anomalies, but in four books, she's never found her way home. I don't know how to write that journey because I've never made it myself.

Until now.

I spend the next hour selecting passages to read, carefully choosing sections that won't reveal too much of my heart. I settle on a chapter from book two where Captain Elian discovers an abandoned library on a distant planet, the last repository of knowledge from a long-dead civilization. It's one of my better pieces of writing, and far enough removed from my current emotional state to be safe.

As I practice reading aloud, my phone buzzes with a text. It's from Lily.

Dad said you're doing an event at our store! So cool! Can I help set up?

I smile despite my anxiety. *Of course. I'll need my biggest fan there.*

Awesome! Dad's actually excited I think. He's been reorganizing the event space like three times.

My heart does a strange little flip. Oliver, excited? About seeing me? No, about hosting an event that will bring in customers, I remind myself sternly.

Tell him not to go to too much trouble. I'm pretty low maintenance.

Too late! He's already ordered special cookies from the bakery that look like your book covers. See you Thursday!

I set the phone down, a complicated warmth spreading through my chest. Special cookies. Reorganizing the space. These small details shouldn't mean anything, but they do. They mean Oliver cares, at least about doing this right.

Whether that's for the store, for Lily, or for some small part of him that remembers us, I don't know. But for the first time since agreeing to this event, I feel something besides panic.

I look back at my list of boundaries and add one final line:

· Be honest about who you are now

The boy who left Harbour Point fifteen years ago doesn't exist anymore. Neither does the boy who was left behind. We're different people now, shaped by the choices we made and the lives we've lived apart. Maybe that's the only way forward—not trying to recapture what we were, but discovering who we are now.

I close the notebook and look at the clock. Almost two in the morning. I should sleep, but my mind is too full of Oliver—the boy he was, the man he's become, the father who orders cookies shaped like my book covers.

Thursday looms ahead, both too far away and too close. I have less than a week to prepare myself to face the man I never stopped loving, in the place where it all began.

Chapter 6

Thomas

Thursday arrives with the kind of perfect coastal weather that makes Harbour Point postcards sell out at the tourist shops—crisp blue skies, gentle breeze, sunlight glinting off the distant water. I dress carefully, trying to thread the needle between professional author and casual returnee. Dark jeans, a blue button-down that Vera, my agent, once told me brings out my eyes, and a sport coat that I can remove if it feels too formal.

I arrive at Harbour Books an hour and a half before the scheduled reading. The "Closed for Event Setup" sign is already hanging on the door, but it swings open when I try the handle. The familiar bell jingles overhead.

"Hello?" I call out, stepping into the renovated space. The store smells exactly as it should—paper, coffee, and that indefinable scent of well-loved books.

"We're in the back!" Lily's voice carries from behind the shelves. I follow it to find the event space transformed from the cozy reading nook I remember to something more polished. Rows of chairs face a small podium, with my book covers enlarged and mounted on foam board displays.

"Mr. Winters!" Lily bounces on her toes, clipboard in hand. "You're early!"

"Thomas, please," I remind her, setting down my messenger bag. "Thought I'd help set up."

"Perfect timing." Oliver emerges from a storage closet carrying a stack of folding chairs. "We could use an extra pair of hands."

He's wearing dark-framed glasses I haven't seen before, and a green sweater that makes his eyes look like forest pools. I swallow hard and force myself to look away.

"Just tell me where you want me," I say, then immediately regret my phrasing as heat creeps up my neck.

"Chairs," Oliver says quickly, nodding toward the stack he's carrying. "We need about twenty more set up."

I nod and move to help him, our hands brushing as I take half his load. The brief contact sends electricity up my arm, and I notice Oliver's sharp intake of breath. We work in silence, unfolding chairs and arranging them in neat rows. The quiet between us pulses with unspoken words.

"Dad, I'm going to check on the refreshments," Lily announces, glancing between us with curious eyes before disappearing toward the café area.

Now it's just the two of us, moving in the space like dancers who know the steps but are afraid to acknowledge the music. I find myself anticipating Oliver's movements—stepping left when he moves right, reaching for the next chair just as he straightens from placing one. Our old rhythm, still there beneath the weight of all the years.

"You've done amazing things with the store," I say finally, needing to break the charged silence.

Oliver looks up, a flash of surprise crossing his features. "Thanks. It's been a process."

"Your father would be proud."

Something softens in his expression. "I hope so. He never got to see it like this."

"How did he...?" I trail off, realizing I don't even know when Mr. Chen passed away.

"Heart attack." Oliver straightens the last chair in his row with precise movements. "It was sudden."

"I'm sorry," I say, meaning it deeply. Mr. Chen had always been kind to me, even if he never knew exactly what I was to his son.

Oliver nods, then changes the subject. "We need to set up the signing table. There's a tablecloth in the supply closet."

I follow him to the familiar door at the back of the event space. When he hesitates before the shelves of supplies, I reach past him without thinking.

"Second shelf from the top, right side," I say, pulling down a folded black tablecloth. "You always kept the display materials together."

Oliver stares at me, something unreadable flickering in his eyes. "You remember that?"

I shrug, suddenly self-conscious. "Some things stick with you."

"Like the way you still tilt your head when you're trying not to say something," he counters softly.

Our eyes meet, and fifteen years compress into nothing. I'm seventeen again, lost in Oliver Chen's gaze, feeling found for the first time.

The moment stretches, breaks when Lily's voice calls from the café. "Dad! The bakery delivery is here!"

Oliver steps back, clearing his throat. "I should get that."

"I'll set up the table," I offer.

He nods and walks away, leaving me with a tablecloth and too many memories.

By the time Oliver returns carrying a box of cookies decorated to look like my book covers, I've arranged the signing table with stacks of my novels, promotional bookmarks, and a jar of pens.

"These are incredible," I say as he sets down the cookies. "You didn't have to go to all this trouble."

"It was Lily's idea," he says, but the careful arrangement of the display tells me he's put thought into this too. "She's your biggest fan."

"One of two in this town, I suspect," I say lightly.

Oliver's hands still on the cookie box. "I've read all your books, Thomas."

The admission hangs between us. I want to ask what he thought of them, if he recognized the pieces of himself I've scattered throughout the stars, if he knows that Captain Elian's most trusted companion—the quiet, brilliant navigator who always finds the way back to their home base—has his eyes.

Instead, I ask, "Even the new one?"

"There is no new one. Not yet." He studies me. "How's it coming along?"

I hesitate, then admit, "It's not. I've been stuck for months."

Oliver's gaze softens, a hint of the old concern I remember so well crossing his features. "That bad, huh?"

"Worse." I run my hand through my hair, a nervous habit I've never shaken. "Vera—my agent—she calls me daily now. The last conversation ended with her threatening to camp outside my rental cottage until I produce something."

"She sounds intense."

"She's already in the stages of planning venues for a book tour." I lean against the signing table, suddenly exhausted just thinking about it. "Fifteen cities in three weeks. Hotel rooms, flights, signing events just like this one but with hundreds of people asking the same questions over and over."

"And you don't want to go," Oliver says, not a question but an observation.

"I used to love it. Meeting readers, hearing their theories about

Captain Elian's next adventure." I gesture around the bookstore. "But now the thought of sitting in places like this, pretending I have answers when I can't even write the first chapter..."

Oliver steps closer, close enough that I can smell the faint trace of his cologne—something woody and subtle. "What happened?"

The genuine concern in his voice nearly undoes me. How do I tell him that what happened was remembering him? That coming back to Harbour Point has made me realize I've been writing the same story for fifteen years—the story of what I lost when I left?

"I think I've been running from something," I admit. "And now Vera's talking about promotional schedules and cover designs for a book that doesn't exist, and I'm just..." I spread my hands helplessly. "Empty."

Oliver studies me for a long moment. "You remember what my father used to say about empty vessels?"

I shake my head.

"They make the most room for new things."

The simple wisdom of it—so like Mr. Chen—makes my throat tight. "Is it just writer's block?"

"Something like that." I run my fingers along the edge of the table. "The series is supposed to be five books. I've known the ending since before I wrote the first one, but now that I'm here..."

"You can't find the words," he finishes for me.

"No. I can't find the heart." I look up at him. "The first four books were about exploring, discovering, pushing boundaries. This one needs to be about coming home, and I don't know how to write that."

Oliver's expression softens. "Because you never have?"

The question cuts straight through me. "Because I left home behind," I say quietly. "Because I'm not sure I deserve to find it again."

His eyes widen, and I see him start to reach toward me, then stop.

"Thomas—"

"Cookie delivery!" Lily bursts into the room carrying another tray of the cookies decorated like book covers. She stops, looking between us. "Am I interrupting?"

"No," Oliver says quickly, stepping back. "Perfect timing."

I force a smile, though my heart is pounding. I came too close to saying too much. "These look amazing, Lily. Did you help design them?"

"I sent them pictures of all your covers," she says proudly, setting down the tray. Her eyes dart between her father and me. "Were you guys talking about the new book? Dad has theories about what happens to Captain Elian."

"Does he?" I look at Oliver, who suddenly appears uncomfortable.

"He thinks she's going to find—"

"Lily," Oliver cuts in, "why don't you finish setting up the refreshment table? People will start arriving in about thirty minutes."

Lily rolls her eyes but complies, taking the cookie tray with her. "Fine, keep your theories secret. But Mr. Winters—Thomas—needs inspiration, Dad."

When she's gone, I turn to Oliver. "Theories?"

He busies himself straightening books that don't need straightening. "Just reader speculation. Nothing important."

"It is to me," I say quietly. "What do you think happens to her?"

Oliver pauses, then meets my eyes. "I think she realizes that exploring the universe means nothing if you don't have someone to share it with. I think she goes back to the beginning to find what she left behind."

My breath catches. "And then?"

"That's your story to write," he says softly. "Not mine."

Before I can respond, Lily returns, clipboard in hand. "The café staff wants to know if they should start serving coffee now or wait until after the reading."

The moment breaks, and Oliver steps away. "I'll go talk to them."

As he leaves, Lily watches him go, then turns to me with knowing eyes. "You two were friends before, weren't you? More than just knowing each other from school."

I choose my words carefully. "We were close, yes."

"He gets this look when he talks about you," she says, arranging cookies on a plate. "Like he's seeing something far away."

"It was a long time ago," I say, though the words feel hollow.

Lily gives me a look that seems too wise for her thirteen years. "Not to him, it wasn't."

* * *

The room fills gradually, then all at once. I stand near the back, watching faces both familiar and foreign filter through the door of Harbour Books. My hometown, turning out to see what became of the boy who left.

"Is that really him?" A woman in her fifties whispers to her companion, not realizing I can hear. "Sarah Chen's husband's old friend?"

Old friend. Such a neat, tidy label for what Oliver and I were.

I scan the crowd, surprised by the turnout. There must be sixty people crammed between the bookshelves, some perched on the windowsills, others standing against walls. Several faces trigger flashes of recognition—my high school English teacher, the librarian who used to slip me advanced reading copies, the barista from the coffee shop where I wrote my college application essays.

Lily darts through the crowd with professional efficiency, directing people to seats, handing out bookmarks with my photo on them. She catches my eye and gives me a thumbs-up.

Oliver appears at my side, startling me. "Bigger turnout than we expected," he says, voice low. "Apparently, you're something of a celebrity here."

"Small-town boy makes moderately good," I joke, but my voice sounds strained even to my own ears.

"Are you nervous?" Oliver asks, studying my face.

I am, but not for the reasons he might think. "It's been a while since I've done a reading."

"You'll be great." His hand hovers near my arm for a moment, as if he might touch me, then drops away. "I've set water on the podium and there's a stool if you prefer sitting."

The thoughtfulness of it—the way he remembers how my legs used to bounce with anxiety when I had to speak in front of our high school English class—makes my chest tight.

"Thank you," I manage.

Oliver nods once, professional and distant, then moves to the front of the room. "Ladies and gentlemen, welcome to Harbour Books. We're honoured to host the New York Times bestselling author Thomas Winters for a special reading and signing tonight."

The crowd applauds, and I feel a strange disconnect as Oliver introduces me with my formal accolades—awards I've won, sales figures, critical acclaim. This is how he knows me now: Thomas Winters, author. Not Tommy, the boy who used to trace constellations on his bare skin.

I take my place at the podium, adjusting the microphone. "Thank you all for coming. It's... surreal to be back in Harbour Point after so long." I clear my throat. "I'd planned to read from one of my latest published novels, but if you'll indulge me, I'd like to share something new instead."

A murmur runs through the audience. I pull out pages I printed just hours ago—not from the manuscript I've been struggling with for months, but from what I started writing that night after seeing Oliver again.

"This is from the opening of what may become my fifth book," I say, though I'm not entirely sure that's true. "It's a work in progress, so you're the first to hear it."

I take a deep breath and begin reading:

"Captain Elian stood at the view port of the Horizon, watching a familiar blue planet grow larger in the darkness. Fifteen years since she'd left, fifteen years exploring the far reaches of uncharted space, and now she was back where it all began. Not by choice—the ship's quantum drive had malfunctioned, forcing an emergency landing at the only spaceport within range. The universe had a cruel sense of humour, returning her to the one place she'd promised herself she'd never see again.

"The planet's night side came into view, and she could make out the coastline she once knew by heart, the curve of the northern peninsula where she'd spent countless nights watching stars with—"

I pause, swallowing hard.

"—with the one person who had made this place feel like home. The one she'd left behind.

"'We'll be docked for repairs within the hour, Captain,' her first officer reported. 'Engineering estimates three days minimum.'

"Three days. Seventy-two hours on a planet with five billion people, only one of whom mattered. What were the odds they'd cross paths? And if they did, what would remain of what they once shared? Fifteen years was a lifetime. People changed. Moved on. Built new lives.

"She had changed too, hardened by the void between stars, by decisions that kept her crew alive but cost pieces of her soul. The person she'd been when she left—young, certain, burning with ambition—was gone. What remained was a captain with a mission, a responsibility to her crew and to the Galactic Confederation.

"And yet, as the spaceport lights came into view, Elian felt something she hadn't experienced in years: the fluttering wings of possibility. Perhaps, in returning to the beginning, she might find what she had been missing all along."

I look up from the pages. The room is silent. My eyes find Oliver, standing at the back of the crowd. His face is carefully composed, but I know him—even after all these years, I know him—and I can see the recognition in his eyes, the slight parting of his lips.

He knows. He knows this isn't just about a fictional captain returning to her home planet. He knows I've written our story into the stars.

"The quantum drive," he murmurs, so softly I barely hear it across the room, but our eyes lock and I know he's remembering the night I first explained my idea for faster-than-light travel in the Captain Elian universe—how we sat on the beach beneath the stars, and I drew diagrams in the sand while he asked questions that made the concept better, stronger.

I continue reading, describing the captain's first steps back onto her home planet, the familiar scent of salt air, the weight of gravity after so long in space. With each word, I feel myself sinking deeper into truth dressed as fiction, and I watch Oliver's face as he recognizes moments from our shared past transformed into science fiction.

When I finish, the applause is immediate and enthusiastic. I set the pages down, hands slightly shaking.

"That was beautiful," says a woman in the front row. "Is this a new direction for the series?"

"I'm... still figuring that out," I admit. "The story is rapidly evolving."

"Will we finally learn who the navigator is based on?" asks another audience member, a bearded man clutching a well-worn copy of my first novel.

The question hits like a punch to the gut. The navigator—Oliver's fictional counterpart—has been a fan favourite since the beginning, the steady presence who balances Captain Elian's impulsiveness, who keeps her tethered when she risks floating away.

"I—" My voice falters. The room suddenly feels too warm, too crowded.

"I believe that's what makes Thomas's work so compelling," Oliver's voice cuts in smoothly. He steps forward, commanding the room's attention. "He creates characters that feel real because they contain pieces of real experiences, but transformed through imagination. Isn't that right, Thomas?"

I nod, grateful for the lifeline. "Yes, exactly. The navigator, like all my characters, comes from... impressions, feelings, connections I've experienced." I meet Oliver's eyes briefly. "Some more significant than others."

"But is Captain Elian based on you?" someone else calls out.

Oliver and I exchange a glance, and I see the hint of a smile touch his lips.

"Captain Elian is braver than I am," I say honestly. "She faces her fears head-on. I've spent most of my life running from mine."

The candid admission silences the room for a moment, until Lily pipes up from where she's perched on a bookshelf.

"What about the ending? Will Captain Elian stay home in the last book?"

Oliver moves closer to the front, our eyes meeting again. "I think what my daughter is asking is whether you believe in second chances, Mr. Winters."

The question beneath the question hangs between us.

"I want to," I say quietly, looking directly at him. "I'm trying to."

The moment stretches, electric and fragile, until another audience member asks about my writing process, breaking the spell. Oliver steps back, resuming his role as bookstore owner rather than... whatever we are to each other now.

The Q&A continues, and I find myself relaxing into the familiar rhythm of discussing my work. Whenever a question throws me, Oliver is there, offering context or redirecting with the natural ease of someone who knows both my work and me intimately.

We function as a team, anticipating each other's thoughts, building on responses. It's effortless, this dance we do, as if fifteen years haven't passed at all.

After the formal portion ends, I sign books for nearly an hour. Oliver manages the line with quiet efficiency, making sure everyone gets their moment without letting anyone monopolize my time. Lily circulates with refreshments, beaming with pride as if she personally discovered me.

Finally, the last customer leaves, and Lily begins collecting empty cups and napkins.

"That went well," Oliver says, closing the front door and flipping the sign to CLOSED.

"Thanks to you," I reply. "You saved me a few times there."

He shrugs. "You would have managed."

"Maybe. But it was better with you."

The words hang between us, heavy with unspoken meaning. Oliver busies himself straightening chairs, avoiding my eyes.

"The new pages," he says after a moment. "They're good, Thomas. Really good."

"They're true," I say quietly. "That's the difference."

He pauses, hands gripping the back of a chair. "Is it? True?"

"You know it is." I step closer. "Oliver, I—"

"Dad!" Lily calls from the café area. "The espresso machine is making that weird noise again!"

Oliver's shoulders tense, then relax. "Coming!" he calls back. He glances at me, something vulnerable flickering across his face before disappearing behind his careful mask.

"I should help her," he says. "And you probably need to get back to your writing."

"Oliver—"

"Thank you for doing this," he cuts me off, professional again. "It was good for the store. For Lily too—she'll be talking about this for weeks."

Just like that, the moment is gone, the almost-confession swallowed back. He steps away, moving toward the café where his daughter waits.

II

Part Two

Chapter 7

Lily

I wait until Dad's flipping pancakes Saturday morning before making my move. Perfect timing—his hands are busy, and the kitchen smells like butter and maple syrup. He can't escape.

"So there's this meteor shower tonight," I say, casually leaning against the counter. "The Perseids. They're supposed to be amazing this year."

Dad flips a pancake with practiced precision. "Is that right?"

"Yeah. The astronomy club at school posted about it before summer break. Peak viewing around eleven tonight at North Beach." I watch his face carefully. "We should go."

His spatula pauses mid-air. "Tonight? I don't know, Lil. It's pretty late for you."

"Dad." I cross my arms. "It's summer vacation. And it's not like I have a bedtime anymore."

"You absolutely have a bedtime."

"Fine, but can we please make an exception? This is science, Dad. Educational. Isn't that what you're always saying I should focus on?"

He slides the pancake onto a plate, his mouth twitching. "Using my own words against me. Clever."

"I learned from the best." I grab the syrup bottle. "Besides, when's the last time we did something fun together? Just us?"

Dad's expression softens. I know it's a low blow—he's been trying so hard since Mom died. Working constantly, making sure I have everything I need. Everything except him, sometimes.

"The beach will be packed," he tries.

"Not if we go to that little cove past the lighthouse." I keep my voice casual, though my heart beats faster. That's where Thomas's cottage is. "It's secluded. Perfect for stargazing."

Dad freezes, spatula hovering over the pan. "The cove?"

"Yeah. Why? Is there something wrong with it?"

"No, it's just..." He pours more batter into the pan. "Nothing. It's fine."

I hide my smile behind my juice glass. Dad's a terrible liar.

"So we'll go?" I press.

He sighs, shoulders dropping in defeat. "Fine. We'll go."

"Yes!" I pump my fist in the air. "You won't regret it, Dad. It'll be awesome."

"I'm already regretting it," he mutters, but there's a smile playing at his lips.

Phase one complete. Now for phase two.

* * *

I wait until Dad's busy with inventory in the back of the store before slipping out. Thomas's cottage is a fifteen-minute bike ride from Harbour Books. I pedal fast, the wind whipping my hair as I rehearse what I'll say.

The cottage sits on a grassy bluff overlooking the cove, weathered grey shingles and blue shutters. I prop my bike against a tree and take a deep breath before knocking.

Thomas opens the door mid-laugh, phone pressed to his ear. His smile widens when he sees me.

"Hey, I've got to go. Call you back," he says into the phone before pocketing it. "Lily Chen. To what do I owe this surprise visit?"

"Are you busy tonight?" I ask, skipping the small talk.

He raises an eyebrow. "Depends who's asking and why."

"There's a meteor shower. The Perseids. Best viewing is at the cove right below your cottage." I point down the path. "You should come."

"Should I now?" His eyes crinkle at the corners. "And who would I be watching these meteors with?"

I shrug, aiming for nonchalance. "Oh, you know. Me. My dad. Maybe some other people from town."

Thomas leans against the door frame, studying me. "Does your father know you're inviting me?"

"He knows we're going to watch the meteor shower." Not technically a lie.

"Mm-hmm." Thomas crosses his arms, but he's smiling. "And you thought I might enjoy tagging along."

"You write about space. Figured you might want to see some real space stuff for a change." I kick at a pebble on his porch. "Plus, I have questions about Captain Elian that only you can answer."

"Ah, now the truth comes out." He laughs. "You're just using me for insider information."

"Maybe. Is it working?"

Thomas shakes his head, amused. "What time?"

"Ten-thirty. We'll be setting up blankets and stuff." I back toward my bike, victory making me bold. "Bring snacks if you want. Dad always forgets."

"Does he now?" Thomas's voice has gone soft.

"Yeah. He gets caught up in the stars and forgets everything else." I swing onto my bike. "See you tonight!"

I pedal away before he can change his mind, grinning into the summer air. Phase two complete.

* * *

Dad checks his watch for the third time in five minutes. "We should get going if we want a good spot."

I look up from my book, hiding my smile. He's been fidgety all afternoon, changing his shirt twice and packing our picnic basket with meticulous care. "It's only nine-forty-five. The shower doesn't peak until eleven."

"Yes, but..." He runs a hand through his hair. "Parking might be an issue."

"We're walking to the cove, Dad. It's like fifteen minutes from here."

He sighs. "Right. Of course."

I close my book and stand, taking pity on him. "But we can head out now if you want. I'll grab the blankets."

We walk in comfortable silence, Dad carrying the picnic basket and telescope, me with blankets and pillows piled high in my arms. The night air smells like salt and pine, and the first stars are appearing overhead.

"You know," Dad says suddenly, "I used to come here a lot. When I was younger."

"To watch stars?"

He nods, eyes fixed on the path ahead. "Among other things."

"With Mom?"

His steps falter. "No. Before I met your mom."

I want to ask more, but something in his voice stops me. Instead, I bump my shoulder against his arm. "Well, I'm glad we're doing it now."

The cove opens up before us, a perfect crescent of sand cradled by rocky cliffs. The water laps gently at the shore, and the lighthouse beam sweeps over the horizon in slow, steady pulses.

"Perfect spot," Dad says, setting down the telescope. "Not too many people yet."

I scan the beach, pretending I'm not looking for anyone specific. "Let's set up over there." I point to a flat section of sand near the path that leads up to Thomas's cottage.

Dad spreads the blankets while I arrange pillows in a comfortable nest. I've just finished when a familiar voice calls out.

"Room for one more stargazer?"

Dad spins around so fast he nearly topples over. "Thomas?"

Thomas stands at the edge of our blanket setup, holding a thermos and a bag of what looks like cookies. He's wearing a dark blue sweater that makes his eyes seem deeper in the twilight.

"Lily invited me," Thomas says quickly. "I hope that's okay?"

Dad shoots me a look that promises a serious conversation later. I smile innocently.

"I ran into him yesterday," I lie smoothly. "Told him about the meteor shower. You don't mind, right, Dad? Thomas writes about space. He should see the real thing."

"Of course I don't mind," Dad says, though his tight smile suggests otherwise. "The more the merrier."

"I brought hot chocolate and snicker doodles," Thomas holds up his offerings. "Homemade. Well, the cookies are store-bought, but I heated them up so they're almost like homemade. And the hot chocolate is from a powder mix, but you can't even tell the difference."

Dad's expression softens slightly. "You didn't have to bring any-thing."

"Lily mentioned you might forget snacks."

"Oh did she?" Dad raises an eyebrow at me.

I shrug. "You get distracted by the stars."

Thomas laughs, and after a moment, Dad joins in. Something in my chest loosens at the sound of their laughter mingling.

"Well, you're not wrong," Dad admits. He gestures to our blanket setup. "Have a seat, Thomas. We've got plenty of room."

Thomas settles on the blanket, careful to leave space between himself and Dad. I position myself on Dad's other side, creating a perfect triangle.

"So," Thomas says, "when do the fireworks start?"

"They're meteors, not fireworks," I correct him. "And probably around eleven. But sometimes you can see early ones."

"I stand corrected." Thomas grins at me. "Meteors it is."

Dad busies himself with the telescope, focusing it on the moon first. "Want to take a look while we wait?" he offers Thomas.

"Absolutely."

I watch as Dad shows Thomas how to adjust the focus, their heads bent close together over the eyepiece. Their shoulders almost touch, and neither seems to notice.

"It's incredible," Thomas murmurs, still looking through the telescope. "Makes you feel small and significant all at once, doesn't it?"

Dad's expression shifts to something I can't quite read. "That's exactly how I've always felt about it."

They exchange a look that makes me feel like I'm intruding on something private. Time for phase three.

I wait until they're deep in conversation about constellations before making my move. I check my phone, then gasp dramatically.

"Everything okay?" Dad asks.

"Yeah, just..." I stand up, brushing sand from my jeans. "Madison and Zoe are here with their parents. They're set up by the lighthouse. Do you mind if I go hang out with them for a bit?"

Dad frowns. "I thought this was our thing tonight."

"It is! But..." I gesture vaguely toward the distant figures I can barely make out in the darkness. "It'll just be for a little while. Please?"

Dad and Thomas exchange glances.

"I don't want to intrude on your family time," Thomas says, starting to stand. "I can head back—"

"No!" I say too quickly. "I mean, you should stay. Keep Dad company while I'm gone. He gets bored easily."

"I do not get—"

"Thanks!" I cut Dad off, already backing away. "I'll be back before the shower's peak. Promise!"

I dart off before either of them can protest, feeling slightly guilty but mostly triumphant. Phase three complete.

From a safe distance, I turn to look back at them. They sit side by side now, no longer maintaining that careful distance. Dad says something that makes Thomas laugh, his head tilting back to the star-filled sky.

I smile and continue toward the lighthouse, where there are indeed some classmates gathering, though I hadn't planned to join them originally. Maybe my little white lie can become truth after all.

The first meteor streaks across the sky, a brilliant flash of silver against the darkness. I make a wish on it, then turn away to give Dad and Thomas their privacy.

Some stars need space to align properly.

* * *

Oliver

The night sky opens above us like a canvas splashed with distant diamonds. I spread the blanket wider on the sand, muscle memory guiding my hands to smooth the corners just as I did fifteen years ago. My fingers tremble slightly, betraying the calm I'm trying to project.

"She really is something else, your daughter," Thomas says, settling beside me on the blanket. Not too close, but close enough that I catch the faint scent of his cologne—different from what he wore as a teenager, but somehow still familiar.

"Yeah." I smile despite my nervousness. "Subtle as a hurricane."

Thomas laughs, the sound carrying across the empty beach. "Wonder where she gets that from."

"Not me, that's for sure." I lean back on my elbows, eyes fixed on the stars rather than the man beside me. "Sarah was the outgoing one. Bold. Said what she meant."

"And you're still the quiet observer." Thomas's voice softens. "Some things don't change."

A meteor streaks across the sky, and we both point at the same moment. Our hands hover in the air, inches apart. I lower mine first.

"Remember when we used to count them?" Thomas asks. "You always saw more than I did."

"I had better night vision." The words slip out before I can stop them, acknowledgement of our shared past hanging in the air between us.

"Still keeping score?" Thomas grins, and for a moment, I see the boy I knew—eager, competitive about the silliest things.

"Forty-seven to thirty-nine, last time." The numbers had stayed with me all these years, tucked away with other memories I'd carefully preserved.

Thomas looks surprised yet pleased. "You remember."

I shrug, trying to appear casual. "Good with numbers."

Another meteor blazes overhead, leaving a trail that lingers before fading. The night is cool but not cold, perfect for stargazing. Perfect for remembering.

"So." Thomas breaks the silence. "The cafe in the bookstore is new."

I swallow hard. "It was struggling. I had to reinvent it or lose it."

"It was genius."

"Sarah's idea, actually." I pick at a loose thread on the blanket. "She had a knack for business. Saw opportunities I missed."

Thomas nods, processing. "And you've been running it alone since..."

"Three years, yeah." I watch another meteor streak by. "Cancer. It was quick, at least. Lily was ten."

"I'm sorry, Oliver." His voice carries genuine pain. "I should have—"

"Don't." I cut him off gently. "You couldn't have known."

We fall silent again, watching the sky. The rhythm of the waves provides a soundtrack to our halting conversation, filling the gaps between words.

"Captain Elian," I say finally. "She's remarkable."

Thomas turns to look at me, surprise evident on his face. "You still remember all the details, even after all these years?"

"Of course I have." I don't add that I bought each one on release day, that I searched for glimpses of us in every adventure. "Your world building is incredible. The Celestial Archipelago in book three? I could see it."

"That was based on the view from—" He stops himself.

"From here," I finish. "I recognized it."

The admission hangs between us. I've just revealed I'd not only read his books but looked for connections to our past in them.

"Have you decided what happens to her?" I ask, changing the subject slightly. "In the fifth book, I mean. Where does Captain Elian go next?"

Thomas sighs, running a hand through his hair. "That's the million-dollar question. My editor's about ready to kill me."

"Writer's block still ongoing?"

"Something like that." He picks up a handful of sand, letting it sift through his fingers.

I sit up straighter, drawing my knees to my chest.

"How much longer are you staying?" I ask, my voice carefully neutral.

"The rental's for two months. After that..." He shrugs. "Depends on whether I find what I'm looking for, I guess."

I want to ask what that is, but I'm afraid of the answer.

"And you?" Thomas turns the question back to me. "Have you ever thought about leaving Harbour Point since back then?"

"No." The answer comes quickly. "This is home. My father's store, Lily's school, our house..." I pause. "Everything I need is here."

"Everything?" His question is gentle, not challenging.

I don't answer directly. "How about you? The famous author life treating you well?"

Thomas laughs, but there's little humour in it. "Famous is a stretch. Moderately successful sci-fi writer with a dedicated but niche following is more accurate."

"You're being modest. I've seen the reviews, the sales rankings."

"You've been keeping that close of tabs on me?" His eyebrow arches.

Heat creeps up my neck. "Professional interest. Bookseller, remember?"

"Right." He doesn't sound convinced.

Another meteor shoots across the sky, brighter than the others. We both watch its path until it disappears.

"New York?" I ask, redirecting.

"Boston, actually. Smaller apartment than you'd expect. View of a brick wall." Thomas stretches his legs out. "Lots of literary parties I mostly avoid."

"Still not a people person?"

"Only with the right people." His eyes meet mine briefly before returning to the stars.

The weight of unspoken words presses on my chest. Fifteen years of silence, of paths diverging and circling back. I wonder if he feels it too.

"Remember when we used to make up constellations?" Thomas points to a cluster of stars. "That was the Cosmic Squid, according to you."

I laugh, surprised he remembers. "And you said it looked more like a spatula."

"We compromised on Spatula Squid."

"A truly undiscovered wonder of the cosmos."

We both laugh, and something loosens in my chest. This is easier than I expected, falling back into our old patterns.

"Oliver." Thomas's voice turns serious. "Can I ask you something?"

My heart stutters. "Sure."

"Are you happy? Here, with your life?"

The question catches me off guard. Am I happy? I have the store, I have Lily. I have a community that respects me, a routine that sustains me. But happiness?

"I'm..." I search for the right words. "I'm content. Lily is healthy and smart. The store is doing well. It's a good life."

"That's not what I asked."

I meet his gaze directly for the first time since we sat down. "Happiness is complicated. I was happy enough with Sarah. I'm happy being Lily's dad. Other kinds of happiness..." I trail off.

"What about you?" I counter. "Famous author living the dream. Are you happy?"

Thomas considers this, his profile outlined against the star-filled sky. "I love writing. Creating worlds, characters. But sometimes I wonder if I'm just hiding in them."

"Hiding from what?"

"Reality. Consequences. The past." He looks at me. "Regrets."

The word hangs between us, heavy with implication.

"We all have those," I say quietly.

Another meteor streaks overhead, and this time we both track it silently.

"You know," Thomas begins, "I never told anyone about—"

"I know," I cut him off quickly, my heart racing. "I know you wouldn't have shared that with anyone."

Relief flashes across his face, followed by something else—hurt, maybe. "Not even my parents. Not my editor. No one."

I nod, watching another meteor streak across the sky. The silence stretches between us, filled with fifteen years of unspoken words.

"Oliver," Thomas says finally, his voice careful, measured. "Can I ask about Sarah?"

My chest tightens at her name. Not from pain exactly, but from the complexity of it all. I knew this question was coming, had rehearsed answers in my head on sleepless nights, but now that it's here, words feel inadequate.

"What do you want to know?" I ask, buying time.

Thomas shifts on the blanket, angling his body toward mine. "How did you... I mean, after we..." He stops, recalibrates. "Were you happy with her?"

I take a deep breath, searching for honesty without cruelty. "It wasn't what you think," I say finally. "Sarah and I, we were friends first. Good friends."

"Friends," Thomas repeats, the word hanging between us.

"She knew about me. About..." I gesture vaguely between us. "She knew I was gay."

Thomas's eyebrows shoot up. "She knew? And she still—"

"It was complicated." I pick up a handful of sand, letting it sift through my fingers. "After my dad's first heart attack, I was lost. The store was struggling. I was drinking too much, staying out late after classes. Sarah was in all the same classes as me."

I close my eyes, remembering Sarah's patient smile, her quiet determination.

"She found me one night, drunk at the community college's campus bar. Took me home, made me coffee, listened to me ramble about everything—the store, my dad, you." I pause. "Especially you."

Thomas is silent, listening.

"We became friends. Real friends. She'd come by the store, help me organize events when my dad wasn't feeling well. We'd grab dinner, watch movies." I smile at the memory. "It was easy with her. No pressure, no expectations."

"But you married her," Thomas says softly.

"Yeah." I look up at the stars. "My dad was getting worse. The medical bills were piling up. I was drowning in debt, about to lose the store. And Sarah..." I swallow hard. "Sarah proposed a solution."

Thomas waits, his expression unreadable.

"She was orphaned in her late teens after her parents died and had family money from the life insurance settlements. Not rich, but comfortable. She offered to help with the store, with Dad's care. Said we made a good team, that we could build something together."

"A marriage of convenience," Thomas supplies.

I shake my head. "No, it was more than that. We did love each other, just not..." I struggle to find the words. "Not in the traditional way."

The memory surfaces, vivid and clear—Sarah sitting across from me at her kitchen table, her hands wrapped around a mug of tea.

"I know you'll never love me the way you loved him," she'd said, her voice matter-of-fact. "And that's okay. I'm not asking for that."

"Then what are you asking for?" I'd replied, confused.

"Partnership. Friendship. Family." She'd reached across the table, her fingers brushing mine. "We're good together, Ollie. We make sense. And I've always wanted a child. You'd make a great father."

"But you deserve someone who—"

"I deserve to choose my own happiness," she'd interrupted. "And this would make both you and me happy."

I blink back to the present, Thomas watching me intently.

"She wanted a family," I continue. "She wanted the store. And I..." I hesitate. "I wanted to stop feeling so alone."

Thomas nods slowly, understanding dawning in his eyes. "So you built a life together."

"We did. It was good, too. Certainly different than what I'd imagined for myself, but good." I smile, remembering. "When Lily was born, Sarah cried. Said it was the happiest day of her life."

"And you?" Thomas asks quietly.

"It was for me too," I admit. "Holding Lily for the first time... nothing compares to that."

Another meteor streaks overhead, leaving a bright trail across the dark sky.

"Sarah was an amazing mother," I continue. "Patient, creative. She read to Lily every night, built blanket forts in the living room, taught her to ride a bike in the park."

"And you were a family," Thomas says, his voice neutral.

"Yes." I meet his gaze directly. "We were."

"I'm glad," he says, and I'm surprised to hear sincerity in his voice. "I'm glad you weren't alone."

"Sarah got sick when Lily was nine," I say, the words coming easier now. "Ovarian cancer. Stage four by the time they caught it."

Thomas winces. "I'm so sorry."

"The doctors gave her three months. She fought for a year." I smile sadly. "Stubborn to the end."

"Like someone else I know," Thomas says softly.

I laugh despite myself. "Yeah, well. Sarah was the strong one. Through chemo, radiation, experimental treatments. She never stopped planning for the future. Redecorating the store, organizing Lily's birthday party from her hospital bed."

I remember the last few months—Sarah growing thinner, her vibrant energy dimming, but her mind sharp as ever.

"Promise me something," she'd said one night, her voice barely above a whisper.

"Anything," I'd replied, holding her hand.

"Don't hide anymore. After I'm gone. Be who you are."

"Sarah—"

"I mean it, Ollie. We had our time. It was good. But don't use me as an excuse to keep hiding. Go be yourself, be happy."

"Lily was incredible through it all," I say, pulling myself back to the present. "Ten years old, and she'd sit by Sarah's bed, reading aloud from your books, actually."

Thomas looks startled. "My books?"

I nod. "Sarah introduced her to Captain Elian when Lily was eight. She loved the space adventures, the strong female heroine. During the worst days, those stories were her escape."

"I had no idea," Thomas whispers.

"After Sarah died, Lily read them over and over. I think..." I pause, considering. "I think they helped her process everything. The idea that even when things seem darkest, there's always another star to navigate by."

Thomas blinks rapidly, looking away. "I wrote those words for you," he says, so quietly I almost miss it.

"I know," I reply simply.

He turns back to me, eyes glistening. "I wanted to resent her when Lily told me about her" he confesses. "The woman who got to have the life I wanted. With you."

The raw honesty in his voice catches me off guard.

"I imagined her as this perfect wife, this perfect match. I told myself you'd moved on already and didn't want to see me." Thomas shakes his head. "God, I was so wrong. So selfish."

"You couldn't have know," I say gently.

"I could have reached out. I could have asked. Maybe if I did, things would be different today" His voice breaks slightly. "Instead, I just... wrote books about escaping. About a captain who never looks back."

"If you did, then I wouldn't have Lily." I say, pausing for a moment. "Either way, she looks back in book four," I point out. "Captain Elian returns to the Celestial Archipelago."

"But doesn't stay," Thomas counters.

"Not yet," I say quietly.

Our eyes meet, and something electric passes between us.

"Sarah knew everything about you," I say, changing the subject slightly. "Not just that you existed, but what you meant to me. She used to tease me about it, actually. Whenever your books came out, she'd buy them first, read them before me. She'd say, 'Your space boy's still thinking about you.'"

Thomas laughs, a short, startled sound. "Space boy?"

"Her nickname for you." I smile at the memory. "She'd point out all the parts she thought were about us. The hidden cove on Proxima B. The run-down old bookstore on the space station in book two."

"She wasn't wrong," Thomas admits.

"I know." I look up at the stars again. "She kept a journal. After she died, I found it. She'd written that she always felt like there were three people in our marriage—her, me, and the ghost of Thomas Winters."

Thomas is silent, processing.

"She wasn't bitter about it," I clarify. "Just... aware. She hoped I'd find the courage to be myself after she died."

"And have you?" Thomas asks quietly. "Found that courage?"

I consider the question, feeling the weight of Sarah's hope, of Lily's future, of fifteen years of choices that led us both back to this beach.

"I'm trying," I say finally. "For the first time since she died, I'm really trying."

Another meteor blazes across the sky, brighter than the others, leaving a trail that seems to linger.

"That's forty-eight to thirty-nine," I say, counting the meteor. "I'm still winning."

Thomas laughs, the tension breaking. "Always keeping score."

We sit in comfortable silence for a moment, watching the stars.

"I never stopped writing to you," Thomas says suddenly. "Every word, every story. They were all letters I couldn't send."

"I know," I say, my voice barely above a whisper. "I always knew."

"Dad!" Lily's voice cuts through the night air. "Thomas! Did you see that huge one?"

I turn to see my daughter jogging back toward us, her face alight with excitement. Whatever Thomas was about to say remains unspoken.

"Perfect timing, kid," I call back, relief and disappointment warring within me. "We just saw it."

Lily drops onto the blanket between us, effectively creating a buffer. "This is so cool. Way better than watching from our backyard."

"The view's always been special here," Thomas says, his eyes meeting mine over Lily's head.

"Can we come back tomorrow night?" Lily asks, looking between us. "The meteor shower peaks tomorrow, right?"

"I don't know, Lil. You have to help me with inventory early the next day, and—"

"Please? It's still summer vacation for another week, I can stay up late for a bit longer!"

I glance at Thomas, who shrugs slightly. "It's fine with me if you want to use the beach again."

"We'll see," I say, the parental standby when I need time to think.

Lily launches into an explanation of meteor science she must have researched online, and I listen with half an ear, my thoughts elsewhere. Sitting here with Thomas feels dangerously comfortable, as if the years between us have compressed into something less significant than they should be.

I look at Thomas as he points out another constellation to Lily, his face animated in the starlight. He's different now—more confident, more polished—but underneath I see glimpses of the boy who used to read me his stories in hushed whispers, who saw things in me no one else bothered to look for.

"Earth to Dad," Lily waves her hand in front of my face. "You're spacing out."

"Just enjoying the night," I say, ruffling her hair. "And thinking."

"About what?" she asks.

I look from her to Thomas, who waits for my answer with careful neutrality.

"About how some things change," I say finally. "And some things stay exactly the same."

Thomas's eyes hold mine for a moment longer than necessary, and I wonder if he understands what I'm not saying.

Another meteor blazes across the sky, and all three of us look up to watch its brilliant, temporary path through the darkness.

Chapter 8

Lily

"Dad, you look exhausted." I lean against the counter as my father rubs his eyes for the third time in five minutes. The morning rush has finally died down, leaving Harbour Books in that peaceful lull before the afternoon browsers arrive.

"I'm fine, Lily." He straightens a stack of new releases that doesn't need straightening.

"You've been up since five. I saw your light on when I got up for water."

His shoulders slump slightly. "Just couldn't sleep."

I don't mention that I know he's been having trouble sleeping ever since the meteor shower three nights ago. Ever since Thomas Winters showed up at our spot on the beach with those ridiculous store bought snicker doodles and that look in his eyes when he saw Dad.

"Why don't you take a break? Go run those errands you've been putting off." I grab the inventory clipboard from behind the counter. "I can hold down the fort."

"I don't know, Lil..."

"Dad. You've been talking about getting those supplies for the bathroom remodel for weeks. Plus, didn't you say you needed to stop by the bank before they close?"

He hesitates, and I can see the internal debate playing across his face. Dad hates leaving the store during business hours, even on slow days.

"I could reorganize the stockroom while you're gone," I add, sweetening the deal. "It's a disaster back there, and you know it."

This gets his attention. The stockroom has been Dad's white whale since we expanded the café section last spring.

"You'd do that?"

I shrug. "Not like I have other plans. Unless you count finishing my summer reading list, which, spoiler alert, I don't."

The corner of his mouth twitches. "You're a strange teenager, you know that?"

"So I've been told." I spin the clipboard in my hands. "So? Deal?"

He checks his watch. "If I leave now, I could be back by two."

"Perfect. That gives me three hours to transform chaos into order." I make a shooing motion. "Go. The store and I will be fine."

Five minutes later, I'm waving from the front window as Dad's car pulls away from the curb. Mrs. Abernathy, our Saturday regular, is already settled in the reading nook with her romance novel and chai latte, and two college students are browsing the poetry section. The store feels peaceful, almost like it's holding its breath.

I flip the sign on the counter to "Ring Bell for Service" and head toward the stockroom, grabbing my water bottle and phone on the way.

The stockroom is exactly as I described it to Dad—a complete disaster. Boxes of new arrivals are stacked haphazardly against one wall, next to towers of damaged books waiting to be returned to publishers. The shelves along the back wall are a jumble of office supplies, promotional materials, and holiday decorations that should have been put away months ago.

"Challenge accepted," I mutter, plugging my phone into the small speaker Dad keeps back here. I queue up my favourite playlist and get to work.

An hour later, I've made impressive progress. The new arrivals are unpacked and sorted by genre, ready to be shelved. The damaged books are boxed properly with return forms paper clipped to each box. I've even tackled the holiday decorations, consolidating three messy boxes into one neatly labelled container.

I'm sweeping the floor when my eye catches on Dad's desk in the corner. Unlike the rest of the stockroom, his desk is meticulously organized—pens in their holder, sticky notes aligned in a perfect stack, computer screen wiped clean. Dad's always been like this with his personal spaces, even when the world around him is in disarray.

I'm about to turn away when something catches my eye. The bottom right drawer of the desk has a small keyhole. In all my years helping around the store, I've never noticed a locked drawer before.

"Weird," I say to the empty room. Dad isn't exactly the type to keep secrets. At least, I didn't think he was.

I try the drawer handle, confirming it's locked. What could possibly be important enough to keep under lock and key in a bookstore stockroom?

The bell at the front counter dings, pulling me away from my discovery. A customer needs help finding a cookbook for their nephew who's heading to college. By the time I ring up their purchase and return to the stockroom, my curiosity has only grown.

I scan the desk for any sign of a key. Nothing in the pencil cup. Nothing taped underneath the desktop—I check, feeling like a spy in one of those movies Dad and I watch on Friday nights. Nothing in the other drawers, which all open easily.

I'm about to give up when I notice the small wooden box on the shelf above the desk. It's hand-carved, with a constellation pattern etched into the lid. I've seen it before but never paid much attention to it. Dad's always had little astronomy-themed decorations around.

Standing on tiptoe, I carefully lift the box down. It's lighter than I expected. The lid opens easily, revealing a small silver key nestled on a bed of faded blue velvet.

My heart beats faster as I pick up the key. This is definitely snooping. If Dad wanted me to see whatever is in that drawer, he wouldn't have locked it.

But then again, he did ask me to organize the stockroom. And technically, the desk is part of the stockroom...

Before I can talk myself out of it, I slide the key into the lock and turn. The drawer opens with a soft click.

Inside is a stack of notebooks—the composition kind with the black and white speckled covers. They look old, the corners worn soft with handling over the years. On top of the notebooks sits a faded blue folder.

I carefully lift out the folder first. Inside are loose pages covered in handwriting I don't recognize—at first. But as I study the neat, compact script with its distinctive way of crossing t's and looping g's, realization dawns.

I've seen this handwriting before. Just last week, in fact, when Thomas Winters signed my copy of "Captain Elian and the Nebula's Heart."

These are Thomas's pages.

My hands shake slightly as I turn to the first page. At the top, in that same handwriting, is a title: "The Navigator's Star." Below it, a dedication:

For O, who showed me the constellations and gave me a universe.

O. My father's name is Oliver.

I sink into Dad's desk chair, my heart pounding. The first page begins:

The navigator traced the star chart with fingers that knew every line by heart. The coordinates for home had never changed, though he had spent years pretending they didn't exist. Sometimes, in the quiet hours between shifts, he would pull out the old chart—the one not logged in the ship's official systems—and remember the boy with eyes like the ocean who had once promised to wait...

I flip through more pages, each one filled with stories about space explorers, distant planets, and impossible journeys. But woven through every narrative are little details that feel personal, intimate. A character who collects first editions of ancient Earth books. A hidden cove on a distant planet where two young explorers share their first kiss under twin moons. A spaceship captain named Orion who keeps a telescope by his window, always pointed toward a particular star.

These aren't just stories. They're love letters barely disguised as science fiction.

With trembling hands, I set aside the folder and pick up the top notebook. The date on the first page reads September 2005—nearly twenty years ago. The handwriting inside is my father's.

Thomas showed me his new story today. I can't believe he made me a spaceship captain. He says I'm brave enough to command a whole fleet, which is ridiculous. But when he talks about the stars like that, I almost believe him.

I close the notebook quickly, feeling like I've stumbled onto something too private, too raw. These aren't just old mementos—they're pieces of my father's heart, carefully preserved and hidden away.

My father and Thomas Winters. They weren't just high school friends who lost touch. They were...together. In love.

Suddenly, so many things make sense. The way Dad tensed up when Thomas first came to the store. How they moved around each other during the book signing, like planets caught in each other's gravity but afraid to orbit too close. The obvious electricity between them at the beach during the meteor shower.

And Thomas's books—all those stories about Captain Elian searching the galaxy, never quite finding what she's looking for. They weren't just science fiction. They were about my dad.

The bell at the front counter dings again, startling me out of my thoughts. I carefully return everything to the drawer, lock it, and place the key back in its wooden box. My mind is racing as I help an elderly couple find a gift for their grandson.

By the time Dad returns at quarter past two, I've finished reorganizing the stockroom and am calmly shelving new releases in the fiction section. He looks better than when he left—some colour has returned to his face, and he's carrying several bags from the hardware store.

"Wow, Lily," he says, poking his head into the stockroom. "This looks amazing. I can actually see the floor."

"Told you I could handle it." I keep my voice casual, though my heart is still pounding. "How were your errands?"

"Productive." He sets his bags down. "I ran into Thomas at the hardware store."

I watch his face carefully. "Thomas Winters?"

"Yes." Dad busies himself with unpacking a bag of tile samples. "He's, uh, having some issues with the plumbing at his rental cottage. I told him which fixtures to buy."

"That was nice of you." I notice the slight flush creeping up my father's neck, the way his hands linger just a moment too long on each tile sample. "You guys seemed to hit it off at the beach the other night."

Dad's movements falter briefly. "We were good friends in high school."

"Just friends?" The question slips out before I can stop it.

His eyes snap to mine, startled. For a moment, I think he might actually answer honestly. Then his expression closes, becoming the careful mask he's worn since Mom died.

"He's invited us for dinner tomorrow night," Dad says instead of answering my question. "At his cottage. To thank us for the book signing and... everything."

"Are we going?"

Dad turns away, arranging tile samples in a neat row. "I told him we would. Unless you don't want to?"

"No, I want to go." I study my father's profile—the tension in his jaw, the careful way he's avoiding my eyes. "I think it would be good. For both of us."

He looks at me then, really looks at me, and for a second I wonder if he somehow knows what I found. If he can read in my face that I've glimpsed the history he's kept locked away all these years.

"Thomas mentioned he might show you some of his notes for the next Captain Elian book," Dad says softly. "He says you have good insights."

"I'd like that." I hesitate, then add, "He's a really good writer. His stories feel... personal. Like he's writing from experience."

Dad's expression shifts, something vulnerable flashing across his face before he masks it again. "The best writers put themselves into their work."

"Dad?" I wait until he meets my eyes. "Are you okay? With seeing Thomas again?"

He takes a deep breath, his fingers tracing the edge of a blue tile that matches the colour of the ocean visible from Thomas's cottage.

"I'm figuring it out," he finally says. "One day at a time."

I nod, deciding to keep my discovery to myself for now. Whatever happened between my father and Thomas Winters is clearly still unfolding. And maybe, just maybe, they deserve the chance to write their own ending.

* * *

Thomas

I stare at my laptop screen, the cursor blinking mockingly at me as I attempt to write. The document is mostly blank—a few paragraphs of half-formed ideas and false starts. My phone vibrates against the wooden desk, pulling my attention away from the emptiness before me.

An email notification. From Alison Bennett, executive editor at Stellar Press.

My stomach drops as I open it.

Thomas,

I've been trying to reach you through Vera for weeks. The silence is concerning. The general director is pressuring me for updates on Captain Elian's final adventure. We need to see what you have. ALL of it. Now.

This isn't a request. Send whatever you have as soon as possible, or we'll need to start discussing contractual obligations and timelines.

Alison Bennett

Executive Editor, Stellar Press

"Shit." I slam my laptop closed and pace the cottage's small living room.

Alison going around Vera means things are worse than I thought. The publisher never contacts authors directly unless something's seriously wrong. Vera's been running interference for months, buying me time, but apparently her goodwill has run dry.

I grab my phone and pull up Vera's number, then stop. What would I even tell her? That I've been writing about Oliver instead of Captain Elian? That I've completely abandoned the space adventure my readers expect for what amounts to a thinly-veiled love letter to my high school heartthrob?

My fingers drum against the kitchen counter as panic rises in my chest. Fifteen years of building my career, and I'm about to throw it all away because I can't get over a relationship that ended when I was eighteen.

I glance at the notebook where I've been scribbling thoughts about Oliver, about us. Those words flow easily. Too easily. But they're not what I'm being paid to write.

The pressure squeezes my lungs until I can barely breathe. I need to produce something—anything—to keep Alison off my back. But every time I try to write about Captain Elian, my mind drifts back to the beach, to Oliver's face illuminated by starlight, to the possibility that maybe, just maybe, we might have a second chance.

* * *

Oliver

I run a lint roller over my navy blue button-down for the third time. A small voice in my head mocks me for caring so much about dinner at Thomas's cottage, but I ignore it.

"Dad, your shirt is fine," Lily calls from the doorway of my bedroom. "We're going to be late."

"Just making sure I look presentable," I mutter, setting the lint roller down and checking my reflection one last time. My hair is neatly combed, face freshly shaved. I look... decent. Professional. Like someone going to a casual dinner with an old acquaintance, not someone visiting the man who once knew every inch of my heart and body.

Lily rolls her eyes. "It's just Thomas. He's seen you covered in meteor shower sand and didn't run away screaming."

"That's different," I say, grabbing my keys from the dresser. "This is his home. It's more... personal."

"Uh-huh." Lily's knowing smirk makes me wonder, not for the first time, if she somehow knows more than she's letting on.

The drive to Thomas's rental cottage takes less than fifteen minutes. My hands grip the steering wheel too tightly as we wind along the coastal road. The setting sun casts long shadows across the pavement, and the ocean glitters gold and orange to our right.

"You know," Lily says casually, "Thomas is really nice."

"Yes, he is."

"And he's single."

I nearly swerve the car into the curb before regaining control. "Lily Chen!"

"What? Just making an observation." She looks out the window, the picture of innocence. "You're single too."

"That's not—we're not—" I take a deep breath. "Thomas and I are old friends reconnecting. That's all."

"If you say so."

We pull up to the cottage just as the last sliver of sun disappears below the horizon. Thomas's rental sits on a small bluff overlooking North Beach, its weathered shingles and white trim glowing in the twilight. Light spills from the windows, warm and inviting.

Before I can even knock, the door swings open.

"You made it!" Thomas stands in the doorway, wearing dark jeans and a soft-looking gray sweater pushed up at the sleeves. His face breaks into a smile that makes my chest ache. "Come in, come in."

The cottage smells amazing—garlic, herbs, something rich simmering. Thomas has transformed the small space into something that feels like home. Books are stacked on every surface, papers and notebooks scattered across the coffee table. A laptop sits open on the kitchen counter next to a bottle of red wine.

"I hope you like pasta," Thomas says, leading us into the kitchen. "It's about the only thing I can cook without burning down the building."

"Pasta's perfect," I say, handing him the bottle of Cabernet I brought. Our fingers brush, and I pull back too quickly, feeling my cheeks flush. "Thanks for having us over."

"Dad makes amazing pasta too," Lily chimes in. "He does this thing with lemon and—"

"Lily," I warn, feeling my face heat up.

Thomas laughs. "I'd love to try Oliver's pasta sometime." His eyes meet mine, and for a moment, I'm seventeen again, sitting cross-legged on the bookshop's floor as he reads me his latest story.

"Can I help with anything?" I ask, desperate to break the moment.

"You can open that wine," Thomas suggests, turning back to the stove. "Glasses are in that cabinet. Lily, would you mind setting the table? Plates are over there."

We move around the small kitchen together, falling into an easy rhythm that feels both new and familiar. Thomas stirs the sauce while I pour the wine. Lily arranges plates and silverware on the small dining table by the window overlooking the ocean.

"This view is incredible," Lily says, peering out at the moonlight reflecting on the water.

"That's why I picked this place," Thomas replies. "It reminds me of..." He glances at me. "Well, it reminds me of home."

Dinner is served family-style—a big bowl of pasta with a rich tomato sauce, garlic bread, and a simple salad. We sit around the table, passing dishes back and forth, and for a moment, it feels like we could be a family. The thought hits me with such force that I have to take a large sip of wine to steady myself.

"So," Lily says between bites, "Dad mentioned you two went to high school together."

Thomas's eyebrows rise. "Did he?"

I stare intently at my pasta. "The subject may have come up."

"Well, your dad and I were in the same grade at Whitman High,"

Thomas explains. "We had English and Physics together almost every year."

"Were you friends?" Lily asks.

Thomas's eyes find mine across the table. "We were."

"Best friends, actually," I add, surprising myself. "Thomas used to hide out in my dad's bookstore after hours to write."

"You did?" Lily turns to Thomas, delighted.

Thomas laughs. "I did. Your dad caught me one night. I thought he was going to call the police."

"Instead, I made him tea and asked to read his stories," I say softly.

"And they were good?" Lily asks.

"They were amazing," I admit. "Even then, I knew he was going to be published someday."

Thomas's expression softens. "Your dad was my first reader. The first person who ever believed in my writing."

"He used to write these incredible stories about space explorers and distant planets," I tell Lily. "He'd read them to me while we—" I stop myself. "While we hung out at the bookstore after closing."

"Is that where Captain Elian came from?" Lily asks Thomas.

He nods. "In a way. A lot of those early ideas evolved into the books."

"Dad collects all your books," Lily says. "All of the special first print limited editions."

I feel my face flush. "Lily..."

"Oh does he?" Thomas looks pleased.

"He has them in a special section in his office above the bookstore," Lily continues, ignoring my warning glare. "And he rereads them all the time."

"I appreciate a loyal reader," Thomas says, his eyes never leaving my face.

The air between us feels charged, like the moment before lightning strikes. I clear my throat and stand up, gathering empty plates.

"Dinner was delicious," I say. "Let me help clean up."

"Leave the dishes," Thomas says, standing too. "I thought we could have dessert on the deck. I picked up some pie from that bakery on Main Street."

"Marie's is still there?" I ask, surprised.

"Some things in Harbour Point never change," Thomas says with a smile.

We carry our wine glasses and plates of apple pie out to the small deck overlooking the beach. The night is clear, stars scattered across the sky like diamonds on black velvet. The sound of waves breaking on the shore below provides a soothing backdrop.

Lily claims the single chair, leaving Thomas and I to share the small bench. Our shoulders brush as we sit down, and I feel the contact like an electric current.

"So," Lily says between bites of pie, "tell me more about high school. Did you guys go to prom together?"

I nearly choke on my wine. Thomas laughs, the sound warm in the cool night air.

"No," Thomas says. "Your dad took Melissa Anderson to prom."

"And Thomas went with Rebecca Taylor," I add.

"The cheerleader?" Thomas laughs. "I'd forgotten about that. She spent the whole night talking about her boyfriend at college."

"You looked miserable," I recall, smiling at the memory.

"I was," Thomas admits. "I would have much rather been with—" He stops, glancing at Lily. "With friends."

A comfortable silence falls over us. Lily finishes her pie and sets her plate aside, looking between us with a thoughtful expression.

"You know," she says suddenly, "there's a science fiction convention in Oakridge tomorrow. Thomas, you should come with us!"

"A convention?" Thomas looks surprised.

"It would be fun," Lily insists. "And I bet people there would love to meet you. Dad and I were planning to go anyway."

I wasn't aware of any such plans, but Lily's forcefully hopeful expression stops me from saying so.

"I don't know," Thomas says hesitantly. "Those events can be a bit overwhelming."

"But you'd have us with you," Lily points out. "Right, Dad?"

They both look at me, waiting. In the moonlight, Thomas's eyes are the same deep blue I remember from summer nights long ago, when we'd lie on the beach and he'd point out constellations.

"Right," I say softly. "You'd have us."

Thomas's smile is slow and warm. "Well, when you put it that way... I'd love to come."

"Great!" Lily claps her hands together. "It starts at ten. We can meet you there."

The rest of the evening passes in comfortable conversation. Lily asks Thomas about his writing process, and he answers patiently, giving her insights I know most fans would treasure. I watch them together, something warm unfurling in my chest.

When it's time to leave, Thomas walks us to the door. Lily hugs him goodbye, which seems to surprise and please him in equal measure.

"Thanks for dinner," I say, lingering in the doorway after Lily heads to the car.

"Thanks for coming," Thomas replies. "It was nice, wasn't it? The three of us?"

"It was," I admit. "Lily adores you."

"She's amazing, Oliver. You already know what I think of her."

"Thanks." I hesitate, then add, "She doesn't usually take to people so quickly."

"Must be the Chen family trait," Thomas says with a small smile. "Her father was pretty tough to win over too."

Our eyes meet, and the years between us seem to compress into nothing. For a moment, I think he might reach for me—or I for him. Instead, I step back, breaking the spell.

"See you tomorrow," I say. "Ten o'clock."

"I'll be there," Thomas promises.

As Lily and I drive away, I can see him in my rear view mirror, standing in the doorway of the cottage, watching until we turn the corner and disappear from sight.

"That was nice," Lily says, breaking the silence. "He's nice."

"Yes," I agree, keeping my eyes on the road ahead. "He is."

"And you like him."

It's not a question, but I answer anyway. "I didn't say that."

"Well" Lily says. "Even if you don't want to admit it, he definitely likes you."

I don't respond, but as we drive through the quiet streets of Harbour Point toward home, I allow myself to imagine, just for a moment, what it might be like to have Thomas Winters back in my life again—not as a memory or a what-if, but as something real and present and possible. The thought is both exhilarating yet terrifying.

Chapter 9

Thomas

I wake before my alarm, anticipation buzzing through me like static electricity. Today I'll spend hours with Oliver and Lily at StellarCon, the regional science fiction convention I'd forgotten was happening this weekend. Lily's invitation had caught me off guard at dinner last night—her bright eyes fixed on me with that same intensity Oliver used to have when he would solve a complex math problem.

"You have to come with us tomorrow," she'd said, not a question but a declaration.

Oliver had flushed then, that familiar pink creeping up his neck as he studied his plate with sudden fascination before agreeing with his persistent daughter.

Now, standing before my bathroom mirror, I debate what to wear. Something professional enough for potential fans but casual enough not to look like I'm trying too hard for Oliver. I settle on dark jeans and a blue button-down that I've been told matches my eyes.

I arrive at the convention centre fifteen minutes early, but Oliver's car is already in the parking lot. My stomach flips as I walk through the glass doors into the lobby filled with cos-players and enthusiasts. A teenager dressed as Captain Elian—complete with the silver insignia I described in book three—passes by, and I smile despite my nerves.

"Thomas!"

Lily waves from across the lobby, bouncing on her toes. Oliver stands beside her, hands in his pockets, wearing a simple grey t-shirt with the Harbour Books logo. I notice for the first time that he's let his hair grow out a bit since I first saw him at the store. It curls slightly at his temples the way it did when we were seventeen. The realization makes a wave of nostalgia pass through me.

"You made it." Oliver's voice is steady, but his eyes betray a nervousness that matches my own.

"Wouldn't miss it." I hold up the convention program. "I haven't been to one of these in years."

"Dad has all the programs from your past appearances," Lily says, earning another blush from Oliver. "He keeps them with your books in that special—"

"Lily." Oliver cuts her off with a gentle warning in his tone. "Let's head inside, shall we?"

The main exhibition hall overwhelms the senses—vendor booths, art displays, and cosplay contests competing for attention. I stay close to Oliver and Lily as we navigate the crowds, occasionally stopping when Lily points out something of interest.

"Oh my god." A young woman freezes in front of us, eyes widening. "You're Thomas Winters."

I smile, extending my hand. "That's me."

"I can't believe it. Your books got me through college." She fumbles in her bag for a convention program. "Would you mind signing this? Captain Elian helped me come out to my parents."

My chest tightens with unexpected emotion. "I'd be honoured."

As I sign, I notice Oliver watching me, his expression unreadable. When I hand the program back, the young woman hesitates.

"I have to ask—will Elian ever find her way back to Vega? The person she left behind?"

The question hits too close to home with Oliver standing right beside me. "I'm working on that answer right now, actually."

"Well, I hope she does." The fan glances between Oliver and me, her gaze curious. "Sometimes going back is the only way forward."

After she leaves, more people notice me. What starts as one autograph becomes a small gathering, and soon convention staff are ushering us to an empty table near the author signing area. Oliver and Lily stand to the side as I sign books, posters, and even someone's tablet case. Though I draw the line at signing a woman's bare chest, much to Oliver's amusement.

"I didn't realize you were this famous," Oliver says during a brief lull.

"I'm not. Not really." I shrug. "Science fiction fans are just passionate."

"Like Dad," Lily interjects. "He has theories about every single one of your characters."

Oliver shifts uncomfortably. "Lily..."

"What? You do! You even wrote them down in your—"

"Let's find the panel on speculative astronomy," Oliver interrupts, consulting the program with sudden interest. "It starts in twenty minutes."

The morning passes in a blur of panels and conversations. I find myself watching Oliver as much as he watches me. He's attentive during discussions about honoured and future technology, asking thoughtful questions that remind me of our late-night conversations in his father's bookstore.

During a panel on alternate realities in fiction, I feel Oliver tense beside me as the moderator discusses paths not taken.

"The multiverse theory gives writers endless possibilities," the panellist explains. "Characters can explore what might have happened if they'd made different choices."

"Like if someone stayed instead of left," Lily whispers, not quite under her breath.

Oliver shoots her a pointed look, but I pretend not to hear, focusing instead on the discussion about quantum storytelling and divergent timelines. Yet I can't help wondering about those other versions of us—the Thomas who stayed in Harbour Point, the Oliver who left with me, the lives we might have built together.

After the panel, Lily announces she's hungry. The food court is packed, but we find a small table near the window. As we eat overpriced convention sandwiches, I notice Lily checking her phone with increasing frequency.

"Everything okay?" I ask.

"Actually..." She stands abruptly. "I just got a text from Zoe. She's here with her mom and wants to show me the art exhibition. Is it okay if I meet up with you guys later?"

Oliver frowns. "I didn't know Zoe was coming."

"Last-minute thing." Lily gathers her backpack. "You two should check out the VR experience. Dad, you said you wanted to try it."

Before Oliver can protest, she's weaving through the crowd, phone clutched in her hand.

"She's not getting any more subtle," Oliver says after a moment of silence.

I laugh, relieved he's acknowledging what we both know. "Gets that from you. You were always terrible at pretending."

"Was I?" His eyes meet mine. "I pretended for fifteen years that I was fine without you."

The directness of his statement steals my breath. We haven't spoken this plainly since the night on the beach.

"I should have stayed," I admit. "Or made you come with me."

"We were kids, Thomas."

"Old enough to know what we wanted."

Oliver looks down at his hands. "I wasn't brave enough then."

"And now?" The question hangs between us.

He doesn't answer directly. "The VR experience is supposed to be good. Should we try it?"

The VR exhibition occupies a darkened corner of the convention hall. We wait in line, maintaining a careful distance between our bodies, though I feel Oliver's presence like a gravitational pull. When it's our turn, we're led to separate pods and fitted with headsets.

"This simulation lets you experience alien worlds from popular science fiction universes," the attendant explains. "Including settings from the Captain Elian series."

I smile at Oliver as our visors come down. "See you on the other side."

The virtual reality is impressive—stars expanding around me, then resolving into the bridge of the Horizon, Captain Elian's ship from my books. Every detail matches what I've described in my novels, from the curved navigation console to the viewport showing distant nebulae.

Then the scene shifts, and I'm standing on Vega, the home planet Elian left behind. The golden fields and twin moons rising over purple mountains—all exactly as I'd imagined when writing. I wrote Vega as a composite of Harbour Point and the future I'd dreamed of building with Oliver.

When the simulation ends, I remove my headset to find Oliver already waiting, his expression thoughtful.

"That was..." he begins.

"Weird?" I offer.

"Familiar." He runs a hand through his hair. "I always pictured Vega differently when reading, but seeing it—it felt like somewhere I'd been before."

We walk toward the exit, needing air after the intensity of the virtual experience.

"That's because Vega really is Harbour Point," I say quietly. "The cove, the lighthouse, even the bookstore—I put them all in there, just dressed up with alien features."

We find ourselves in a quiet hallway away from the main convention floor. Promotional posters for upcoming sci-fi films line the walls—alternate worlds and possible futures surrounding us.

"Everything I've written has been about us in one way or another," I confess. "About what I lost when I left. Captain Elian is braver than I was, smarter than I was, but she made the same mistake. She left someone who loved her because she thought the universe was calling."

Oliver leans against the wall. "But she found amazing things out there. Just like you did."

"Not the thing that mattered most." I step closer. "In the fifth book, she's supposed to come home. I've been trying to write it for months, but I couldn't figure out how until I came back here."

"And now?"

"Now I know she needs to ask for forgiveness. She needs to see if there's still a place for her in the love she left behind's life, even after all this time."

Oliver's eyes search mine. "And if there is?"

"Then she stays." My voice drops to a whisper. "She finally stays."

The convention sounds fade around us as Oliver's hand finds mine, our fingers intertwining like they used to when we were teenagers hiding from the world.

"Dad! Thomas!" Lily's voice breaks the moment. She hurries toward us, excitement radiating from her face. "They just announced a special screening of the Captain Elian animated pilot! It starts in ten minutes!"

Oliver doesn't let go of my hand as Lily approaches, and the significance of this small act isn't lost on me. She notices our linked hands and unsuccessfully tries to suppress a smile.

"Sorry, am I interrupting something?"

"Yes," Oliver says simply. "But it's okay. We have time."

The way he says it—like a promise rather than a platitude—makes my chest ache with possibility.

"So, the screening?" Lily prompts, practically bouncing.

"Lead the way," I tell her, still holding Oliver's hand as we follow her through the convention centre.

* * *

Oliver

Thomas's hand feels warm against mine as we sit in the darkened theatre, waiting for the Captain Elian animated pilot to begin. I can't believe I'm here with him after all these years, at a science fiction convention of all places. The last time we'd been to one together, we were seventeen and had saved for months to buy tickets.

"Dad, I'm going to grab some popcorn before it starts," Lily whispers, already sliding out of her seat.

"Do you want me to come with you?" I ask, half-rising.

She rolls her eyes. "I think I can handle the concession stand on my own."

As she disappears up the aisle, Thomas leans closer. "She's remark-able. So independent for someone her age."

"Sometimes too much for her own good," I say, but pride swells in my chest. "Sarah always encouraged that in her."

The lights dim further, and a hush falls over the audience. Thomas doesn't move his hand away from mine, and I don't pull back either. The contact anchors me as the familiar theme music fills the theatre.

The pilot is beautiful—the animation fluid and expressive, capturing the essence of Thomas's world. Captain Elian appears on screen, her confident stride and determined expression exactly as I'd always imagined. And then her navigator appears, a tall man with dark hair and quiet intensity, standing at her side.

"That's Chen" a voice whispers loudly from behind us. "The navigator."

My heart stutters. I glance at Thomas, who's watching me instead of the screen, his expression unreadable in the darkness.

When the episode ends and the lights come up, Lily is still nowhere to be seen. People around us begin discussing the show animatedly, and I overhear a conversation that makes my blood freeze.

"The relationship between Captain Elian and Navigator Chen is my favourite part of the books," a woman in Elian cosplay says to her friend. "He's the emotional anchor to her wild spirit. So loyal and steady."

"Winters really knows how to write that quiet, deep love," her friend agrees. "Remember in book three when Chen refuses to leave the ship during the Andromeda crisis? 'The stars may change, but my place is here with you.' I cried for days."

Thomas's hand tightens on mine. "Oliver—"

"There you two are!" A young woman with a convention badge approaches us. "Mr. Winters, we have a panel discussion about character development in fifteen minutes. Would you and your friend like to join us? We'd love to have the real-life inspiration for Navigator Chen participate."

The floor seems to drop from beneath me. "I'm sorry, what?"

The woman's eyes widen. "Oh! I just assumed... I mean, Thomas Winters has mentioned in interviews that Navigator Chen was based on someone special from his hometown. And when I saw you two together..." She trails off, looking mortified.

"I think there's been a misunderstanding," I manage to say, pulling my hand from Thomas's.

"My fault entirely," she stammers. "Please forget I said anything. Mr. Winters, the panel is in Room 12B whenever you're ready."

She hurries away, leaving an awkward silence between us.

"Oliver," Thomas begins, "I can explain—"

"How many people know?" My voice sounds strange even to my own ears. "How many people have read about us and made the connection?"

"It's not like that. I never used your name in interviews. I never—"

"But you told them Chen was based on someone real? Someone from your hometown?" The convention hall suddenly feels too crowded, too loud. "Our hometown isn't exactly New York City, Thomas."

"Dad?" Lily appears, holding a large popcorn. "What's wrong?"

"Nothing," I say automatically. "I just remembered there's an issue at the bookstore. Mrs. Feldman called while you were gone." The lie slips out easily. "I need to head back."

"But we just got here," Lily protests. "And Thomas has another panel—"

"You can stay if you want. I'll send an Uber for you later." I'm already standing, gathering my jacket. "Thomas, I'm sure you understand."

His face falls. "Oliver, please don't—"

"I'll call you," I say, knowing I won't. Not until I've processed this. "Enjoy the rest of the convention."

I walk away before either of them can respond, pushing through crowds of cos-players and fans, many clutching Thomas's books to their chests. Books that apparently contain pieces of me, of us, that I never consented to share.

Outside, the cool air hits my face, and I gulp it down. How many readers have pictured Navigator Chen and imagined me without knowing it? How many have analyzed his relationship with Captain Elian, dissecting feelings I thought were private between Thomas and me?

The old fear rises in my throat like bile. In high school, I'd been terrified of anyone discovering I was gay, of my traditional Chinese father finding out about Thomas and me. Even after Dad died and I inherited the bookstore, even after marrying Sarah who knew and accepted me completely, I'd kept that part of myself quiet. Small towns have long memories.

And now? Now there are hundreds of thousands—maybe millions—of readers who know some version of our story.

I drive home in a daze, the bookstore excuse forgotten. Once inside, I go straight to my bedroom and pull Thomas's books from my shelf. I've read them all multiple times, of course, but always as science fiction adventures, as the work of the boy I once loved.

Never so explicitly as our story.

I open the first novel, "The Starship Aurora," and begin reading with new eyes.

Navigator Chen stood at the helm, his steady hands guiding the ship through the asteroid field. "There's a safe passage here," he said quietly. "Trust me, Captain."

Elian studied his profile, the determination in his dark eyes. She'd known him less than a month, yet somehow he'd become essential to her crew—to her. "Show me the way home, Navigator."

I remember Thomas reading me this passage years ago, before it was published, before he left for college. I'd thought it was just good writing. Now I see myself in every line.

Hours pass as I flip through all four books, finding us on every page. In the second book, when Chen teaches Elian to navigate by the stars of his home world. In the third, when they're stranded on a frozen planet and share body heat to survive. In the fourth, when Chen refuses a promotion that would separate them.

Our first kiss transformed into their first shared breath in space suits. Our secret swimming spot at the cove reimagined as an alien lagoon where they shelter during a storm. The night Thomas told me he was leaving for college becomes Elian's temporary reassignment to another quadrant.

It's all there—beautiful, painful, and exposed.

"Dad?" Lily's voice startles me. I hadn't heard her come home. She stands in my doorway, looking at the books spread across my bed. "Are you okay?"

"I'm fine," I say automatically. "How did you get home?"

"Thomas drove me." She hesitates. "There wasn't really an emergency at the bookstore, was there?"

I sigh, closing the book in my lap. "No. I'm sorry I lied."

She comes to sit beside me, picking up one of the novels. "These are all about you and Thomas, aren't they?"

My head snaps up. "What do you mean?"

"I found his old manuscript in your desk drawer. 'The Navigator's Star.'" Her voice is quiet. "And I heard what that convention lady said about Navigator Chen."

A wave of emotions crashes over me—embarrassment, fear, but also relief. No more secrets from my perceptive daughter. "How long have you known?"

"I suspected when I first met him. The way he looked at you when he came to the bookstore that day." She traces the cover of the book. "Then I found the folder in your office and knew for sure. You two were in love back then."

"Yes," I admit. "We were."

"And now?"

I look down at the book in my hands, at the story of us that Thomas has been telling the world all these years. "I don't know, Lily. It's complicated."

"Because you're both men?" she asks bluntly.

"Partly," I say. "But also because fifteen years is a long time. We're different people now."

"You remember what Mom said right? She'd want you to be happy now." Lily leans against my shoulder. "Thomas makes you happy. I can see it."

"He also hurt me," I say softly. "And apparently told our story to millions of readers without my knowledge."

Lily picks up another book. "Did you ever ask him why he wrote these?"

"No, not in as many words."

"Then maybe you should." She stands up. "I'm going to bed. Thomas said to tell you he's sorry, and he'll be at the cottage if you want to talk."

After she leaves, I continue reading, unable to stop myself. In the quiet of my bedroom, surrounded by books filled with our thinly disguised love story, I finally understand what Thomas has been trying to tell me.

Every word was a letter he couldn't send. Every adventure, a memory he couldn't let go. Every moment between Captain Elian and Navigator Chen, a wish for what might have been.

The question is: what do I want now?

Chapter 10

I'm staring at the last sentence I wrote hours ago—"Captain Elian traced the familiar constellations of her home world, wondering if she'd made the right choice in returning"—when three sharp knocks cut through the cottage's silence.

My heart stutters. It's nearly midnight. I close my laptop, padding across the wooden floor in socked feet, half-expecting to find a lost tourist asking for directions or maybe Lily with another of her impromptu visits.

But when I swing open the door, Oliver stands on my porch, backlit by moonlight, his shoulders rigid with tension.

"Oliver?" I step back instinctively. "Is everything okay? Is Lily—"

"She's fine. Asleep." His voice is controlled, too controlled. "We need to talk."

I recognize that look—the tightly wound composure that means he's fighting to keep something volcanic contained. I've only seen it a handful of times in all our years together, but it's unmistakable.

"Come in." I hold the door wider, my stomach dropping as he brushes past me.

Oliver doesn't sit. He paces into the living room, turns to face me, and pulls something from his jacket—a worn paperback of my second novel. He holds it up like evidence.

"Navigator Chen discovers the ancient star charts in the temple ruins, knowing the coordinates could save Captain Elian but might cost him everything he's built on Vega." He quotes the passage with perfect recall. "Sound familiar, Thomas?"

I close the door slowly, buying seconds to compose myself. "Oliver—"

"The hidden cove. The night we found those old navigation charts in your grandfather's attic." His voice cracks slightly. "You promised me you'd take me with you someday."

The memory hits like a physical blow. Seventeen years old, sprawled across my grandfather's dusty floor, tracing possible routes across faded star maps while Oliver calculated theoretical travel times.

"You put our entire relationship in these books." He's not asking. "Every moment. Every promise."

"Not every moment," I say quietly.

"Enough." He tosses the book onto my coffee table. "Fifteen years, Thomas. Fifteen years watching you turn us into something you could sell."

The accusation lands like a slap. "That's not what I did."

"No? Then what would you call it? Because from where I'm standing, you left, became famous writing about us, and never once asked me if I was okay with it."

"You were married!" The words burst out louder than I intended. "What was I supposed to say? 'Hey, Oliver, just thought you should know I've been processing our breakup through science fiction that's making me rich and famous while you built a family with someone else?'"

Oliver's eyes flash. "You could have said something. Anything. Instead, I had to piece it together from your books, wondering if I was imagining things or if Captain Elian's navigator was really supposed to be me."

"He was always you." I can't hold it back anymore. "Every word.

Every mission. Every planet they explored together. It was all just... us in a different universe. One where I didn't leave you behind."

"But you did leave." Oliver's voice drops dangerously low. "You left, and then you used what we had for your career."

"I wasn't using us," I step closer, desperate to make him understand. "I was trying to keep us alive the only way I knew how."

"By turning me into a character who follows your protagonist across the galaxy?" His laugh is bitter. "A supporting role in your success story?"

"No! By creating a world where we stayed together!" The confession tears out of me. "Where we got to be what we promised each other. Captain Elian and Navigator Chen exploring the stars together—it was the life we planned before everything fell apart."

Oliver's breathing changes, his anger momentarily displaced by something more complex. "You think that makes it better? That you were writing some fantasy version of us?"

"I think it was the only way I could handle losing you." I sink onto the arm of the sofa. "The first book... I wrote the rough draft in my dorm room, crying most nights, missing you so much I couldn't breathe. Captain Elian wasn't some calculated career move. She was how I survived."

The silence stretches between us, filled with fifteen years of unspoken words.

"You know what I did after you left?" Oliver finally says, his voice eerily calm. "I tried to be exactly what everyone expected. The dutiful son. The straight guy. The husband. The father." His eyes meet mine, filled with a pain that steals my breath. "I folded myself into smaller and smaller spaces until I couldn't remember who I was before I started pretending."

"Oliver—"

"Sarah knew from the beginning that I was gay, that I was still in love with you. She offered me friendship, partnership. A way to stay in Harbour Point without having to explain why I wasn't dating women." His hands tremble slightly. "We built something real together. Something good. But it was never... I was never..."

"Complete," I finish for him.

He nods once, sharply. "And all that time, I kept your books on my nightstand, reading about Captain Elian and her navigator, telling myself it was just because I was proud of you."

I cross the room slowly, stopping just short of touching him. "I came back to Harbour Point to finish the series. But I couldn't write the ending because I didn't know how our story was supposed to end."

"You're the writer," he says, but the edge has left his voice. "You could have written any ending you wanted."

"That's the problem." I risk reaching for his hand, relief flooding me when he doesn't pull away. "I only ever wanted one ending. The one where we found our way back to each other."

Oliver's eyes close briefly, his fingers tightening around mine. "You can't just write us a happy ending, Thomas. Real life doesn't work that way."

"I know." I step closer until I can feel the heat of him. "That's why I came home. Because I needed to know if there was any chance that we could—"

I don't finish before Oliver's free hand slides behind my neck, pulling me forward until our foreheads touch. We stand like that, breathing each other's air, the tension between us transforming into something electric.

"I was so angry when I realized," he whispers. "Not just that you used our stories, but that you understood exactly what it felt like. All these years, I thought I was alone in missing what we had."

"Never." My voice breaks on the word. "I wrote four books trying to find my way back to you."

I'm not sure who moves first—maybe we both do—but suddenly his mouth is on mine, and fifteen years dissolve like morning fog. His lips are both familiar and new, the same softness I remember but with a confidence that makes my knees weak. I grip his shirt, pulling him closer as the kiss deepens from tentative to desperate.

Oliver pushes me backward until I hit the wall, his body pressing against mine as his hands frame my face. "I shouldn't want this," he breathes against my mouth. "I shouldn't still want you."

"But you do." I kiss him again, harder. "We both do."

His fingers thread through my hair, tugging just enough to make me gasp. "Fifteen years, Thomas. Fifteen years wondering what could have been."

I slide my hands under his shirt, feeling the warm skin of his back. "We don't have to wonder anymore."

The look he gives me—hungry, vulnerable, terrified—nearly stops my heart. "This isn't fiction. We can't just skip to the happily ever after."

"I don't want to skip anything." I pull him toward the hallway. "I want every moment. Every conversation. Every argument. Everything we missed."

Oliver hesitates for only a second before following me, his fingers interlaced with mine. "Lily will have questions."

"We'll answer them together." I stop at my bedroom door, suddenly uncertain. "If that's what you want."

His answer is to kiss me again, walking me backward until my legs hit the bed. We tumble onto it, a tangle of limbs and half-removed clothing. I pull his shirt over his head, my breath catching at the sight of him—older, different, but still unmistakably my Oliver.

"You're still beautiful," I whisper, tracing the line of his collarbone.

His smile is shy, almost boyish. "So are you."

We take our time rediscovering each other, though patience quickly gives way to hunger. I unbutton Oliver's shirt with trembling fingers, revealing the canvas of his chest—broader now, dusted with hair that trails enticingly downward. When I drop to my knees before him, his breath hitches audibly.

"Fifteen years," I murmur, mouthing him through his jeans, feeling him harden against my lips. "I've dreamt about tasting you again."

Oliver's head falls back as I unzip him, freeing his straining erection. He's thicker than I remember, the head already glistening with need. I run my tongue along the underside, savouring his salt-sweet flavour and the deep groan it pulls from his throat.

"Christ, Thomas," he hisses when I take him fully into my mouth, my lips stretching around his girth. His fingers thread through my hair, not guiding but anchoring himself as I hollow my cheeks and take him deeper.

I work him with practiced devotion, one hand cupping his heavy sac, the other gripping his thigh to steady myself. When his breathing turns ragged, he suddenly pulls away, hauling me to my feet.

"Not like that," he growls, spinning me toward the bed. "Not this time."

He strips me efficiently, rough palms sliding over each newly exposed inch of skin. When I'm naked beneath him, he pauses to retrieve lube from the nightstand—my preparedness making him raise an eyebrow.

"Hopeful?" he asks, slicking his fingers.

"Desperate," I correct, spreading my legs in shameless invitation.

The first breach of his finger makes me arch off the bed. The second has me clutching at the sheets. By the third, I'm begging incoherently, my cock leaking against my stomach as he expertly works me open, finding that spot that makes my vision blur.

"Please, Oliver," I pant, rocking against his hand. "I need you inside me. Need to feel you."

He withdraws his fingers, leaving me empty and aching. I watch through half-lidded eyes as he slicks himself generously, his cock jutting proudly from the nest of dark curls between his thighs. The sight alone nearly undoes me.

When we're both finally positioned, Oliver hovers above me, the blunt head of his erection pressing insistently at my entrance. His eyes search mine, dark with desire but still questioning. "Are you sure about this? About us?"

I reach up to touch his face, tracing the lines that weren't there when we were boys, then wrap my legs around his waist, urging him forward. "I've never been more sure of anything. Captain Elian always finds her way back to Navigator Chen. It's the truest thing I've ever written."

He laughs softly, pressing his forehead to mine as he pushes forward, the initial penetration burning sweetly as my body yields to him. "You're still a hopeless romantic."

"Only for you," I gasp as he sinks fully into me, stretching me in ways I'd forgotten, filling an emptiness I'd carried for fifteen years. My body clenches around him, drawing him deeper. "It's always been only for you."

Oliver establishes a devastating rhythm, each thrust driving deeper than the last. I wrap my arms around his shoulders, meeting him halfway, our bodies remembering this dance despite the years between. The sound of skin against skin fills the room, punctuated by our mingled moans and half-formed words.

"Touch yourself," Oliver commands, his voice wrecked with pleasure. "I want to watch you come apart for me."

I obey, wrapping my hand around my neglected cock, stroking in time with his increasingly erratic thrusts. The dual sensation is overwhelming—Oliver hitting that perfect spot inside me while my hand works my shaft, thumb swiping through the wetness at the tip.

"I'm close," I warn, feeling the familiar tightening at the base of my spine.

"Look at me," Oliver demands, his pace faltering as he nears his own release. "I want to see your eyes when you come."

Our gazes lock, and it's this intimacy more than the physical pleasure that pushes me over the edge. I come with his name on my lips, my release painting hot stripes between our bodies as I clench around him. Oliver follows seconds later, burying himself to the hilt as he pulses inside me, marking me as his once more.

He collapses against me, our sweat-slicked bodies sliding together as we struggle to catch our breath. I feel him softening inside me but make no move to separate, wanting to prolong our connection for as long as possible.

And as we lie tangled in the aftermath, his seed slowly leaking from me, I know I've finally found the ending to my story—not in the stars, but right here in Harbour Point, in the arms of the man I never stopped loving.

* * *

Oliver

I wake to sunlight streaming through unfamiliar curtains and the gentle sound of waves breaking against the shore. For a moment, I'm disoriented—this isn't my bedroom. Then warmth shifts beside me, and memories of last night flood back.

Thomas.

He sleeps peacefully, one arm flung above his head, hair tousled against the pillow. The sight of him steals my breath. Fifteen years of separation, and now here we are, as if the universe finally aligned.

I study his face—the lines at the corners of his eyes that weren't there in high school, the slight stubble along his jaw. He looks both exactly the same and completely different from the boy I loved. The man I still love.

The realization doesn't frighten me like it once would have.

Thomas stirs, eyes fluttering open. When he sees me, a slow smile spreads across his face.

"You're still here," he whispers, voice rough with sleep.

"Did you think I'd run?"

"Wouldn't have blamed you." His fingers find mine beneath the sheets. "We have a lot to figure out."

I nod, suddenly uncertain. Last night was about re-connection, about fifteen years of pent-up longing finally released. But morning brings reality, complications, questions.

"Coffee?" Thomas asks, sitting up.

"Please."

While Thomas moves around the kitchen, I borrow his shower. The hot water helps clear my head, but anxiety creeps in. What happens now? I have a life in Harbour Point—the bookstore, Lily. Thomas has his career, his life in Boston.

When I emerge, Thomas hands me a steaming mug. We move to the deck, the morning air crisp against our skin as we settle into Adirondack chairs overlooking the water.

"I need to apologize," I say after a long silence.

Thomas looks surprised. "For what?"

"For how I reacted at the convention. Walking out like that." I grip my mug tighter. "It was just... overwhelming to finally acknowledge that I've been living in your books all these years without fully knowing, while the rest of the world knew about me."

"I should have told you sooner." Thomas sets his coffee down. "But I was afraid. Those books—they're the only way I could keep you with me."

"I understand that now." I take a deep breath. "I've spent so long hiding, Thomas. Even from myself. After Sarah died, I just... existed. For Lily's sake."

"And now?"

"Now I don't want to hide anymore." The words feel monumental as they leave my mouth. "I'm gay. I've always been gay. Sarah knew—she was my best friend before anything else. We built a life on friendship and mutual respect, and I loved her, just..."

"Not the way you loved me?" Thomas's voice is gentle, without accusation.

"Not the way I love you," I correct him, meeting his eyes. "Present tense."

Thomas reaches for my hand, our fingers intertwining.

"What about Lily?" he asks.

"She's smarter than both of us combined. I think she's been playing matchmaker." I laugh softly. "Sarah and I never hid anything from her. I'm pretty sure she knows I'm gay, though we haven't talked about it directly."

"And us? What would this even look like, Ollie?"

The nickname makes my heart contract. No one's called me that since him.

"I don't know," I admit. "You have your life in Boston. I have the bookstore here."

"Actually..." Thomas shifts in his chair. "My lease is up next month. I've been thinking about relocating somewhere quieter to finish the series."

Hope blooms in my chest, dangerous and fragile.

"Are you saying—"

"I'm saying I'm open to possibilities." His eyes hold mine. "For the first time in fifteen years, I feel like I'm writing the right story."

We talk for hours, untangling years of separation, discussing practicalities, fears, hopes. It's tentative but real—the careful foundation of something we're both afraid to name yet.

When I finally glance at my watch, I jump up.

"I need to get home. Lily will be wondering where I am."

Thomas walks me to my car, hesitating before I open the door.

"When will I see you again?"

I smile. "Come for dinner tonight. At our place."

"Are you sure?"

"I'm done hiding, Thomas. That includes from my daughter."

His kiss is brief but full of promise. As I drive away, I glance in the rear view mirror to see him standing in the driveway, watching me go. This time, it doesn't feel like an ending.

* * *

The house is quiet when I enter. I check my watch—10:17 AM. Lily's probably still asleep; teenagers and Sunday mornings are a predictable combination.

I move through the kitchen, starting coffee, trying to look casual in yesterday's clothes. My mind races with how to explain this to Lily. Though she's been pushing us together, there's a difference between theoretical matchmaking and your father actually spending the night with someone.

"Dad?"

I turn to find Lily in the doorway, hair mussed from sleep, eyes narrowed with curiosity.

"Morning, sweetheart." My voice comes out unnaturally high.

She studies me, taking in my rumpled shirt and the guilty flush I can feel spreading across my face.

"You're wearing the same clothes as yesterday." A smile tugs at the corner of her mouth. "And you look... different."

"Different how?" I busy myself with mugs, avoiding her gaze.

"Happy." She slides onto a bar stool at the counter. "You stayed at Thomas's place, didn't you?"

I nearly drop the coffee pot. "Lily, I—"

"Dad." She rolls her eyes. "I'm thirteen, not three. I know what's going on."

Setting the coffee down, I take a deep breath and face my daughter. "Yes, I stayed at Thomas's. We had a lot to talk about after... everything."

"And?"

"And what?"

"Are you guys together now?" Her directness catches me off guard.

"We're... figuring things out." I study her expression, searching for discomfort or confusion. "How do you feel about that?"

Lily considers this, tilting her head. "Mom would be happy for you."

My throat tightens. "You think so?"

"She told me once that everyone deserves their great love story." Lily reaches for the mug I've poured her. "She said yours would be complicated."

"Sarah was the best friend I ever had," I say softly.

"Besides Thomas."

"Besides Thomas," I agree. "But she was my family, Lily. You both were—are. That doesn't change."

"I know." She sips her coffee, making a face at the bitterness. "So is he coming over again?"

"Actually, I invited him for dinner tonight. If that's okay with you?"

Her face lights up. "Can we make lasagne? Thomas mentioned it's his favourite."

I laugh, relief washing through me. "When did he tell you that?"

"At the convention. We talked a lot while you were freaking out about being Navigator Chen at home."

"I wasn't freaking out," I protest weakly.

"Dad, you literally ran away." She grins. "It was very dramatic."

"Fine. I freaked out a little." I reach over to ruffle her hair. "But I'm done with that now."

"Good." She hops off the stool. "Because I like him. And you're different around him—more alive."

As she disappears upstairs, I stand in the kitchen, overwhelmed by my daughter's perception and acceptance. For three years, I've worried about failing her, about the void Sarah's death left in our lives. It never occurred to me that in trying to protect Lily, I was teaching her that happiness comes second to safety.

* * *

Thomas arrives at six, bearing flowers and a bottle of wine, this time a Sauvignon Blanc. He looks nervous standing on our porch, shifting his weight from foot to foot. It's endearing to see the confident author so unsure of himself.

"You didn't need to bring anything," I say, taking the wine.

"Actually, I did." He hands me the bouquet. "I'm trying to make a good impression."

"You already have." I nod toward the kitchen where Lily is setting the table. "She's been cooking all afternoon."

Thomas's eyes soften. "She never fails to impress, Ollie."

"Never," I hesitate, then lean forward to kiss him briefly my lips tingling at the contact. "Come in."

Dinner is surprisingly easy. Lily dominates the conversation, peppering Thomas with questions about his books, his writing process, his favourite sci-fi movies. Thomas answers everything thoughtfully, never talking down to her. I watch them interact, this strange new family configuration taking shape before my eyes.

"So I've been thinking," Lily says as we finish the lasagne. "If Thomas is going to be around more, we should clear out the guest room. It's basically just storage now anyway."

I nearly choke on my wine. "Lily, that's—"

"A great idea," Thomas finishes, his eyes meeting mine over the table. "But I think your dad and I need to figure some things out first."

"Like what?" She looks between us. "You love each other, right?"

The directness of her question hangs in the air. Thomas waits, letting me take the lead.

"Yes," I say finally. "But relationships are complicated, especially when they involve history and—"

"Adults always make things more complicated than they need to be," Lily sighs dramatically. "If you love each other, the rest is just details. You're an author, you should know this."

Thomas snorts and begins to laugh. "She has a point, Ollie."

"Don't encourage her," I mutter, but I'm smiling too.

After dinner, Lily insists on handling cleanup alone. "You two go talk or whatever. I've got this."

We retreat to the living room, settling on opposite ends of the couch. The space between us feels significant.

"She's playing matchmaker again," I say, shaking my head.

"Successfully, it seems." Thomas's smile fades into something more serious. "I've been writing again. All day, actually."

"Captain Elian?"

He nods. "The final book. It's... different from what I planned."

"How so?"

"It's about coming home. About the captain and the navigator finding their way back to each other after all these years apart." His eyes meet mine. "I think I finally know how their story ends."

"How?"

"Together." He moves closer on the couch. "If that's what you want too."

I reach for his hand, remembering the boy who once shared his stories with me in the back of my father's bookstore, who named a spaceship after me, who carried our love story into the stars when we couldn't have it on Earth.

"I want that," I whisper. "I want us."

From the kitchen doorway, Lily watches with a satisfied smile before quietly slipping away, leaving us to write the next chapter of our story together.

Chapter 11

Thomas

The cursor blinks on my screen, no longer my enemy but a companion in creation. Words flow from my fingertips like water breaking through a dam—unstoppable, powerful, and clear. For weeks, I've been struggling with Captain Elian's final journey, but now the story unfolds with an inevitability that feels like coming home.

I pause to stretch my back, gazing out the cottage window at the sunlight dancing across the waves. Three hours of uninterrupted writing and I've produced more than I have in months. The truth is, finding Oliver again has unlocked something in me—not just my heart, but my voice.

My phone buzzes with a text from Oliver: *Bringing sandwiches. Be there in 20.*

A smile spreads across my face as I save my work. These lunch breaks have become the highlight of my days. I tidy up the cottage, clearing away coffee mugs and straightening the manuscript pages I've printed for Oliver to read.

When the knock comes, it's gentle but confident—just like him. I open the door to find Oliver holding a paper bag from the café at Harbour Books, his cheeks slightly flushed from the walk.

"Hey," he says, a small smile playing at his lips.

"Hey yourself." I step aside to let him in. "How's the morning rush?"

"Manageable. Left Lily in charge of the register. She's surprisingly good with the customers." He sets the bag down on the kitchen counter and begins unpacking sandwiches. "How's the writing?"

I can't contain my excitement. "I wrote thirty pages this morning. Thirty good pages."

Oliver's eyebrows lift. "That's... impressive."

"It's you." The words tumble out before I can stop them. "Being with you again—it's like I finally remember what I'm writing about."

A blush creeps up his neck as he busies himself with unwrapping our lunch. "Can I read them?"

"That's why I printed them out." I gesture to the stack of papers on the coffee table. "Navigator Chen finally confronts Captain Elian about why she left their homeworld."

Oliver carries our sandwiches to the couch and picks up the pages. "Should I read while we eat?"

"Please." I settle beside him, our shoulders touching. "Your opinion matters more than anyone's."

He takes a bite of his sandwich, then wipes his fingers carefully before turning to the first page. I watch his eyes move across the words, catching every subtle reaction—the slight furrow of his brow, the quick intake of breath, the way his lips part slightly at certain passages.

I try to eat, but my appetite is secondary to my need for his reaction. I wrote these pages with him in mind—every word a confession, every scene a memory transformed.

"This is different," he says after a few minutes. "Your voice is... clearer somehow."

"Different how?"

"It's less... guarded." Oliver turns a page. "Like you're not hiding behind the metaphors anymore."

I nod, understanding exactly what he means. "I'm not."

He continues reading, occasionally pausing to take a bite of his sandwich or sip his water. I've finished eating and sit quietly, watching him absorb my words.

When he reaches the scene where Navigator Chen tells Captain Elian that she waited—that she kept their star chart all these years—Oliver's breath catches.

"This part..." He taps the page. "This isn't how it happened with us."

"No," I admit. "It's how I wished it happened."

He picks the manuscript back up. "This dialogue here—it's beautiful, Tommie. Raw in a way your other books weren't."

"Because I'm not afraid anymore." I shift closer to him on the couch. "I'm not writing for an audience or for my editor. I'm writing for us."

Oliver continues reading, and I watch his face change as he reaches the scene where Navigator Chen reveals that he never stopped loving Captain Elian, even when their paths diverged across galaxies.

"Is this true?" Oliver asks quietly, his finger resting on the paragraph.

"Every word."

He finishes the last page and sets the stack down carefully. "You've found your ending."

"Not yet." I take his hand in mine. "But I'm getting closer."

Oliver checks his watch and sighs. "I should get back. Lily can handle a lot, but the afternoon delivery is coming."

"Tomorrow?" I ask.

He nods. "Same time. I want to read what happens next."

After he leaves, I return to my laptop, fingers hovering over the keys. The cottage feels emptier without him, but his presence lingers in my mind as I begin to type again.

* * *

The next day, I wake before dawn and write straight through the morning. The words come faster now, urgent and honest. I'm no longer writing science fiction—I'm writing our story, thinly veiled in stars and spaceships.

By the time Oliver knocks on my door, I've printed another thirty pages.

"That's... a lot," he says when he sees the stack.

I hand him a cup of coffee made exactly how he likes it—one sugar, splash of cream. "I couldn't stop."

He settles into what has become his spot on the couch, balancing his lunch on his knee and the manuscript in his hand. I sit across from him in the armchair, pretending to check emails while secretly watching his every reaction.

"This scene," he says after a while, "where they're in the observatory and Navigator Chen shows Captain Elian the new star maps he's created during her absence..."

"Yes?"

"It's us at the cove, isn't it? The night before you left for college."

I nod. "You remember."

"Of course I remember." His voice is quiet. "You promised you'd come back."

"I did come back. Just... fifteen years too late."

Oliver's eyes remain on the page, but I can see the emotion in them. "Not too late."

He continues reading, occasionally making small sounds of recognition or surprise. When he reaches the part where Captain Elian confesses that every planet she discovered, she named after something that reminded her of Navigator Chen, Oliver looks up.

"Is that true? In your books?"

"Check the star charts in the appendices. Chenwood. Oliveria. Harbour Point 7. They're all there."

Oliver's eyes widen. "How did I miss that?"

"Most readers think they're random names. Only you would know."

He shakes his head, a mix of wonder and something like regret crossing his face. "All this time, you were sending me messages."

"I was leaving breadcrumbs, hoping somehow you'd find your way back to me." I move to sit beside him. "Or I'd find my way back to you."

Oliver returns to the pages, reading faster now. When he finishes, he sets them down carefully.

"The scene where they finally kiss again—after all those years..." He hesitates.

"Yes?"

"You haven't written it yet."

I take his hand. "Because I'm still living it."

Oliver glances at his watch and stands reluctantly. "I need to get back."

"Take the pages with you," I offer. "Read them tonight."

He gathers the manuscript carefully. "I will."

At the door, he pauses. "Tom?"

"Yes?"

"Write the kiss."

After he leaves, I return to my laptop and begin typing.

* * *

Days blend together in a rhythm of writing and Oliver's visits. My editor calls, surprised and delighted by the sample chapter I've sent.

"This is what we've been waiting for," she gushes. "The depth, the emotion—it's all there. What changed?"

"I got around my writer's block," I tell her simply.

Oliver arrives precisely at noon, a different book from my series tucked under his arm each day. He's rereading them all, he explains, now that he knows what to look for.

Today, he brings *The Stellar Compass*, my second novel.

"Page 247," he says as he settles on the couch. "Navigator Chen's monologue about waiting for the right moment to plot a course home."

I nod, remembering exactly what I wrote. "That was the year I almost came back."

"What stopped you?"

"Fear." I hand him today's pages. "I convinced myself you'd moved on."

Oliver takes the manuscript, our fingers brushing. "I had moved on, in a way. But not from you."

He begins reading, and I watch his face. Today's pages include the scene where Captain Elian and Navigator Chen finally acknowledge the lost years—not with regret, but with understanding that their separate journeys were necessary.

"This part," Oliver says, pointing to a paragraph. "Where Navigator Chen says he needed to build something of his own before he could truly be Elian's partner... that's beautiful, Tom."

"It's true, though. You built Harbour Books into something amazing. You raised Lily. You created a life that's wholly yours."

"And you created worlds." Oliver taps the book he brought. "Literal worlds."

"For you," I remind him. "Always for you."

He continues reading, and when he reaches the scene where Navigator Chen shows Captain Elian the hidden room in the ship's library where he's kept every transmission she ever sent, Oliver's eyes grow misty.

"The drawer in my office," he says softly. "Lily found it."

"The one with my early stories?"

He nods. "And letters. And that terrible poem I wrote you for your eighteenth birthday."

"I loved that poem."

"It didn't rhyme."

"It wasn't supposed to."

Oliver laughs, the sound warming the cottage. "You were always too kind about my writing."

"And you were always exactly what I needed as a reader." I move closer. "You still are."

He finishes the pages and looks up at me. "You wrote the kiss."

"I did."

"It's perfect." He sets the manuscript down. "Is that how you remember our first kiss?"

"Every detail."

Oliver checks his watch and sighs. "I should go."

But today, he doesn't move immediately. Instead, he leans forward and places his hand on my cheek. "Write what happens next, Tom."

His kiss is soft, brief, and carries the promise of more. Then he's gone, leaving me with the taste of possibility on my lips and words crowding my mind, demanding to be written.

My phone vibrates against the desk, jolting me from Captain Elian's world. Vera's name flashes on the screen. I consider letting it go to voicemail, but that would only delay the inevitable.

"Thomas Winters, literary recluse," I answer.

"Thomas Winters, contractually obligated author who owes me pages," Vera counters without missing a beat. "Please tell me you're not still staring at a blank document."

I glance at my laptop screen, filled with words that have been flowing effortlessly since Oliver came back into my life. "Actually, I've been writing."

"Hallelujah. Send me what you have. Now."

"Hello to you too, Vera. Yes, the weather here is lovely. The town is charming."

She sighs. "I've been fielding calls from the publisher all week.

They're talking legal jargon at me again which is never a good sign."

"I just emailed you the first three chapters," I tell her, hitting send. "Fresh off the digital press."

"Hold on." The line goes quiet except for the faint sound of typing. I imagine her in her Manhattan office, glasses perched on her nose, scanning my words with the critical eye that's helped shape my career.

Minutes pass. I pour myself more coffee and wait.

"Thomas," she finally says, her voice different now. "This is... this is what we've been waiting for."

"You think so?"

"I know so. The depth here—it's like you've finally let Captain Elian be vulnerable. And Navigator Chen... there's something different about him in these pages."

I smile to myself. "I suppose I found my inspiration."

"Whatever you found, don't lose it. I'm forwarding these to the publisher immediately. This will buy you some time, but you need to keep this momentum going."

"I will."

"Promise me, Thomas. No more writer's block."

I look out the window toward Harbour Books, where Oliver is probably shelving new releases or helping a customer find their next favourite story.

"No more blocks," I promise. "The words are finally coming."

"Good. I need the next six chapters by Friday."

"You'll have them."

* * *

Lily

I slide the final book back onto the shelf and stand back to admire my handiwork. The science fiction section at Harbour Books has never looked better—alphabetized, colour-coded by series, and with all of Thomas's books displayed prominently at eye level. Dad would be proud, though he's been too distracted lately to notice much about the store.

Not that I mind. The dreamy look Dad gets whenever Thomas comes around is worth a little neglect of the family business. With the cafe side of things booming these days we can afford it.

My phone buzzes with a notification from the Young Writers of America website. The annual competition deadline is in three months, and I haven't written a single word. I've been planning to enter since last year when Ms. Peterson handed me the flyer and said, "Lily, with your imagination, you could win this."

I sink into the reading nook by the window, pull out my notebook, and flip to a blank page. The cursor in my mind blinks mockingly against the white space. I've had ideas swirling around for months—fragments about a girl who discovers she can communicate with stars, each one containing the memory of a different civilization. But whenever I try to pin the words down, they scatter like startled birds.

"Just write something," I mutter to myself. "Anything."

The bell above the door chimes, and I look up to see Mrs. Abernathy shuffling in with her weekly romance novel list. I tuck my notebook away and slip behind the counter.

"Good morning, Mrs. Abernathy! Dad's out getting coffee, but I can help you find what you're looking for."

After helping Mrs. Abernathy and two other regular customers, I retreat to Dad's office during a lull. The deadline looms larger in my mind. The grand prize includes publication in Speculative Horizons magazine and a writing workshop with established authors. I could meet other writers my age who understand what it's like to have worlds trapped inside your head, begging to be released.

I open a new document on Dad's computer and type: "The Star Whisperer by Lily Chen." I stare at the title for five full minutes before deleting it. Too obvious. Too childish.

The office door creaks open, and Dad pokes his head in. "Hey, bookworm. Thomas is coming over to help me organize the author event calendar. Want to join us?"

"Sure." I close the document without saving. "I'll be right out."

When Thomas arrives thirty minutes later, he brings the scent of ocean air and coffee with him. He and Dad immediately fall into their familiar rhythm—talking closely, laughing at inside jokes, their hands finding excuses to touch. It's like watching two planets that have been spinning in separate orbits finally align.

"Lily, your dad tells me you've been running the store single-handedly these past few weeks." Thomas settles into the chair across from me at the small table where we've spread out calendars and contact information for potential visiting authors.

"Someone has to while he's busy making heart eyes at you." I grin as Dad's face flushes.

"Lily Chen!" Dad protests, but Thomas just laughs.

"Fair enough." Thomas winks at me. "But seriously, that's impressive. When I was your age, I could barely remember to feed my goldfish."

"Did you have a goldfish?" I ask.

"No, which explains a lot about why I wasn't trusted with responsibilities."

We work through the calendar, marking dates for upcoming releases and potential events. Thomas's phone buzzes with an email from his editor, and he excuses himself to take a call outside. Dad goes to help a customer, leaving me alone at the table.

I pull out my notebook again, flipping past pages of half-formed ideas and character sketches. Without thinking, I start writing:

The stars speak if you know how to listen. Not in words, but in pulses of light that translate to emotions in your mind. Mira discovered this on her thirteenth birthday, when grief over her mother's death opened something inside her that had always been dormant.

"That's a killer opening line."

I snap my notebook shut, heart racing as I look up to see Thomas standing behind me. "I—it's nothing. Just doodling."

"Doesn't look like nothing." He slides back into his seat. "Mind if I take a look?"

My instinct is to clutch the notebook to my chest and run, but something in his expression stops me. There's no judgment there, no adult condescension. Just genuine interest.

"It's really rough," I warn, slowly pushing the notebook toward him.

"All first drafts are rough. You should see mine—they're disasters." He opens to the page where I was writing and reads silently.

I watch his face for any flicker of disappointment or that polite smile adults get when they're about to say something is "nice" or "interesting" when they really mean it's terrible.

Instead, his eyebrows lift slightly, and he nods as he reads. "This is good, Lily. Really good."

"You're just saying that because you're dating my dad."

"I'm saying it because it's true." He taps the page. "Your character Mira has a unique ability that's connected to her emotional state— that's solid world building. And starting with her mother's death gives her immediate emotional depth."

Heat rises to my face. "It's for this competition. Young Writers of America. The deadline's in three months, and I haven't gotten past this paragraph."

"Writer's block?"

"More like writer's concrete wall. I can see the story in my head, but when I try to write it down…" I trail off, frustrated.

"What happens next? After Mira discovers she can hear the stars?"

I hesitate, then the words tumble out. "She realizes each star holds memories from different civilizations across the universe. And there's this one particular star that keeps showing her memories of her mother—but her mother isn't human in these memories. She's from somewhere else."

Thomas's eyes light up. "That's fascinating. So it's about identity and connection across vast distances."

"Yeah, and about how grief can open doors we didn't know existed." I look down at my hands. "I just don't know if I can write it well enough."

"You can." Thomas slides the notebook back to me. "The Young Writers competition, huh? I entered that when I was sixteen."

"Did you win?"

"Came in third. But that was enough to convince me I might actually have a shot at this writing thing." He leans forward. "Tell you what—if you want, I could take a look at your story as you work on it. Give you some feedback."

"You'd do that?"

"Of course. Every writer needs a first reader. Your dad was mine, back in the day."

I glance toward the front of the store where Dad is chatting with a customer, his hands animated as he recommends a book. "I know, I saw the notebook you wrote for him."

Thomas pauses momentarily, blushing, before continuing. "He has a good eye. Catches things I miss every time."

I consider Thomas's offer. Having a professional author review my work is intimidating, but also exactly what I need. "Okay. But you have to be honest. No sugar-coating because I'm a kid or because of Dad."

"Deal." Thomas extends his hand, and we shake on it. "How about you email me what you have so far, and I'll send you some notes? Then we can meet to discuss."

"I don't have much yet."

"Start with what you've got. Sometimes you need to write the middle before you can figure out the beginning."

Dad returns, sliding his arm around Thomas's shoulders. "What are you two conspiring about?"

"Lily's entering the Young Writers competition," Thomas says before I can answer.

Dad's eyes widen. "Really? That's fantastic! Why didn't you tell me?"

"Because I haven't actually written anything yet," I mumble.

"She's being modest," Thomas cuts in. "She's got a compelling concept about a girl who can hear memories stored in stars."

Dad's face softens with pride. "That sounds amazing, Lily."

"Thomas offered to help me with it," I add.

"Well, you couldn't ask for a better mentor." Dad squeezes Thomas's shoulder. "Though I hope you're charging a reasonable fee. Maybe dinner at our place tonight?"

Thomas laughs. "Sounds fair."

The rest of the afternoon, I catch myself smiling whenever I think about my story. For the first time, it feels like more than just an idea—it feels possible.

That evening after dinner, while Dad cleans up in the kitchen, Thomas and I sit in the living room with my laptop open between us.

"I wrote a little more after you left," I admit, pulling up the document.

"Let's see it."

I turn the screen toward him, holding my breath as he reads:

The stars speak if you know how to listen. Not in words, but in pulses of light that translate to emotions in your mind. Mira discovered this on her thirteenth birthday, when grief over her mother's death opened something inside her that had always been dormant.

The first star that spoke to her was Sirius, its voice a deep blue pulse that filled her mind with images of oceans on a planet circling a distant sun. Creatures with translucent skin and thoughts like liquid silver moved through those waters, building cities of living coral.

But it was the small, unremarkable star in the Cassiopeia constellation that changed everything. When Mira opened herself to its light, she saw her mother's face—not as she remembered her, but transformed. Her mother's skin shimmered with an iridescence no human possessed, and her eyes held the wisdom of centuries.

"Mom?" Mira had whispered to the night sky. "Is that really you?"

The star pulsed once in response, and Mira understood with sudden clarity that the answer was both yes and no.

Thomas finishes reading and looks up at me. "This is really good, Lily. You've got natural instincts for pacing and imagery."

"Really? It doesn't sound stupid or childish?"

"Not at all. It's intriguing and emotionally resonant." He points to a line. "I especially like this bit about thoughts like liquid silver. That's the kind of specific, unexpected description that makes writing come alive."

Pride blooms in my chest. "I wasn't sure if that made sense."

"It makes perfect sense. The best science fiction creates sensory experiences we've never had but can somehow still imagine." He pauses. "I do have a few suggestions, if you're open to them."

"That's why I showed you."

"You might consider starting with a specific scene—maybe Mira looking up at the stars on her birthday—before revealing her ability. Sometimes it helps to ground the reader in a concrete moment before introducing the speculative elements."

I nod, already seeing how that could work. "What else?"

"Think about what Mira wants, beyond understanding these messages. What's driving her forward? What's at stake?"

"She wants to know if her mother is still alive somehow, in another form," I say slowly, the story expanding in my mind. "And she's afraid of what she'll discover—both about her mother and about herself."

"That's perfect." Thomas smiles. "You've got the heart of your story right there."

Dad appears in the doorway, leaning against the frame with a dish towel in his hands. "How's the master class going?"

"Your daughter is talented," Thomas says, looking up at him. "Reminds me of someone else I knew at her age who had a knack for storytelling."

Dad raises an eyebrow. "I never wrote fiction."

"No, but you always knew how to make the world sound more interesting than it was." Thomas's voice softens. "You made me believe I could write stories worth reading."

They share one of those looks that makes me want to simultaneously roll my eyes and cheer. I clear my throat. "I'm still here, you know."

Dad laughs. "Sorry. Continue with your literary genius."

"Actually," Thomas says, "I think we've covered enough for tonight. Lily, why don't you work on expanding what you have, maybe try writing that opening scene we discussed, and email it to me when you're ready?"

"Okay." I save the document and close my laptop. "Thanks, Thomas. This really helps."

Later that night, after Thomas has gone home with a lingering kiss to Dad at the door (which I pretended not to see from the staircase), I sit cross-legged on my bed with my notebook open.

I write until my hand cramps, the story flowing more easily than it ever has before. Mira takes shape on the page—stubborn, curious, afraid of what the stars are telling her but unable to stop listening. By the time I finally fall asleep, I've written eight pages, and for the first time, I believe I might actually have a chance at this competition.

More importantly, I have a story I want to tell, and someone who believes I can tell it.

* * *

Oliver

I lean against the door frame, coffee mug warming my hands as I watch Thomas and Lily hunched over her notebook at our kitchen table. They've been at it for nearly an hour, their heads close together, Thomas pointing at something on the page while Lily nods eagerly.

"The memories aren't just recordings," Thomas says. "Think about what it means that Mira can access them. What does she learn about herself?"

"That she's connected to something bigger." Lily's voice rises with excitement. "That even though her mom is gone, there's still this... continuity."

Something catches in my chest. I take a sip of coffee to push it down.

Thomas glances up, catches me watching them. His smile hits me like sunlight after rain—immediate, warming. "Your daughter's story is incredible, Ollie."

"She gets her creativity from her mother." The words slip out before I can stop them.

"And her determination from you," Thomas counters.

Lily rolls her eyes. "I'm right here, you know."

I laugh, but there's a strange ache beneath it. Seeing them together like this—Thomas mentoring Lily, Lily soaking up his guidance—it's everything I could want. And yet.

"I need more paper," Lily announces, pushing back from the table.

She disappears upstairs, leaving Thomas and me in momentary silence.

"You okay?" Thomas asks quietly.

I move to the table, set my mug down. "It's good. Seeing you two. It's good."

"But?"

I trace the wood grain with my finger. "Sarah would've loved this. You helping Lily with her writing."

Thomas reaches across the table, his fingers brushing mine. "Is that what's bothering you?"

"No. Yes." I shake my head. "I'm happy, Thomas. Happier than I've been in years. But sometimes it feels like I'm building something new on ground that still shifts beneath me."

"The foundation's solid, Ollie. You and Lily—what you two have built together—that's unshakable."

"And where do you fit in all this?" I ask, my voice barely audible.

Thomas's eyes hold mine. "Wherever you'll have me."

Chapter 12

Lily

I tug at my sweatshirt sleeve, trying to ignore the whispers from Zoe and Maddie at the next lunch table. They're not even trying to be subtle, glancing over at me every few seconds like I've grown a second head overnight.

"It's definitely true," Zoe says, just loud enough for me to hear. "My mom saw them holding hands at Rosie's Diner yesterday."

"But isn't her dad, like, married?" Maddie whispers back.

I stab my fork into the cafeteria's sad excuse for mac and cheese. News travels fast in Harbour Point. It's been exactly nine days since Dad and Thomas started officially dating, and somehow the entire town seems to know.

"My mom died three years ago," I announce, turning to face them directly. "And yes, my dad is dating Thomas Winters. The author. Any other questions?"

Their eyes widen, and they turn away quickly, suddenly fascinated by their lunch trays. I turn back to my food, but my appetite is gone. I shouldn't care what people think. Dad is happy—happier than I've seen him in years. Thomas makes him laugh, brings colour back to his face. What's wrong with that?

"Hey, space cadet."

I look up to find my friend Ellie sliding onto the bench across from me, her tray loaded with extra fries.

"Heard you just shut down the gossip twins." She pushes her fries to the middle of the table for us to share. "Nice work."

"It's stupid," I mutter. "Why does anyone care who my dad dates?"

"Because it's Harbour Point and nothing interesting ever happens here." Ellie shrugs. "Except when famous sci-fi authors move to town and fall in love with local bookstore owners who everyone previously thought was straight."

I can't help but smile. When she puts it that way, it does sound like something from a book.

"Seriously though, you okay?" Ellie asks, her voice softer.

"Yeah. It's just weird having everyone suddenly interested in my family."

"Well, I think it's cool. Thomas Winters is basically your stepdad now. Do you get advance copies of his books?"

"It's not like that," I say, though I'm not sure what it is like. Dad and Thomas haven't exactly discussed labels or the future with me. They're just... together. "And yes, I've read parts of the new book already."

Ellie's eyes light up. "No way! What happens to Captain Elian?"

I'm about to answer when Jake Collins walks by our table, making exaggerated kissing noises.

"Hey Chen, does your dad know any other gay guys? My uncle's looking."

My face burns hot. Ellie stands up immediately. "Shut up, Jake."

"What? I'm just asking. Her dad's suddenly into dudes after being married to a chick. Maybe it's contagious."

"My dad was always gay," I say through clenched teeth. "And it's not contagious, you idiot."

Jake laughs. "Whatever. It's weird. One day he's normal, next day he's—"

"He's what?" I stand up now too, hands balled into fists. "Finish that sentence. I dare you."

A teacher notices the commotion and walks over. "Everything okay here?"

Jake shrugs innocently. "Just talking, Ms. Peterson."

"Well, talk somewhere else. The bell's about to ring."

Jake walks away, but not before giving me a look that says this isn't over. I sit back down, my lunch completely forgotten now.

"Ignore him," Ellie says. "He's just jealous because your life is interesting and his peaked when he learned to tie his shoes."

I try to laugh, but something cold has settled in my stomach. What if this is just the beginning? What if things get worse for Dad because of me? Because I encouraged him and Thomas to be together?

I already saw what happened this morning at the bookstore. Dad pretended not to notice when the Henderson family—weekly customers for years—walked past the store windows, glancing in but continuing to the chain bookshop across town. Or when the church book club cancelled their monthly reservation of the reading nook with a terse email.

As I walk through the halls between classes, conversations stop and start around me like faulty light switches. Mrs. Peterson, my English teacher, squeezes my shoulder as I pass.

'Your dad's bookstore is my favourite place in town,' she says quietly. 'That won't change.'

The kindness in her eyes makes my throat tight. But not everyone is like Mrs. Peterson. Principal Harmon avoids eye contact when I pass his office, though he's known Dad for years.

* * *

After school, I head straight to Harbour Books. The familiar bell chimes as I push open the door, and for a moment, everything feels normal again. Dad's behind the counter, glasses perched on his nose as he checks inventory on the computer. Thomas is nowhere to be seen—probably at his cottage writing.

"Hey, kiddo," Dad says, looking up with a smile. "How was school?"

"Fine." I drop my backpack behind the counter. "Just the usual."

He studies my face for a moment too long, and I know he can tell something's off. But before he can ask, the bell chimes again, and Mrs. Hoffman walks in with her book club friends.

"Oliver!" she calls, too loudly for the small space. "Just the man we wanted to see."

Dad straightens up, putting on his professional bookstore owner face. "Ladies, what can I help you with today?"

"We're looking for our next book club selection," Mrs. Hoffman says, but her eyes are scanning the store. "We heard Thomas Winters might be here today."

"He's working at home," Dad says. "But I can recommend several titles—"

"Oh, that's too bad," one of the other women cuts in. "We were hoping to meet him. You two are quite the talk of the town."

Dad's smile tightens slightly. "I'm sure I can help you find a good book. What genre are you interested in?"

But Mrs. Hoffman isn't deterred. "It must be nice having a famous author around. So... unexpected after Sarah. We all thought you'd never—"

"Dad," I interrupt, unable to stand it anymore. "I need help with the new display."

Dad looks relieved. "Ladies, please browse. I'll be right back."

He follows me to the young adult section, where I pretend to rearrange books.

"You okay?" he asks quietly.

"Shouldn't I be asking you that? They're being so nosy."

He sighs. "Small town. It'll blow over."

"But doesn't it bother you?"

"I'm more concerned about you. What happened at school?"

I shrug. "Nothing important."

"Lily…"

"Just some stupid comments from some idiotic boys. It's fine."

Dad looks pained. "I'm sorry. I didn't think about how this might affect you at school."

"Don't be sorry," I say fiercely. "I'm not."

But after he returns to help the book club ladies, I wonder if maybe we should all be more careful. Maybe Thomas shouldn't come to the store so often. Maybe they shouldn't hold hands in public. Maybe—

"Excuse me."

I turn to find a woman I don't recognize standing in the sci-fi section. She's holding one of Thomas's books.

"You're Oliver's daughter, right?"

I nod cautiously.

"I was just wondering… these rumours about him and Thomas Winters. Are they true?"

Something snaps inside me. "They're not rumours. They're dating. And they're happy."

"Oh." She looks surprised at my directness. "It's just… it seems so sudden. After your mother and all."

"My mother died three years ago," I say, my voice steadier than I feel. "And she would want my dad to be happy."

"Of course, dear, but with another man? Don't you find that… confusing?"

I take a deep breath. "The only confusing thing is why everyone cares so much about who my dad loves. Thomas makes him happy. He helps me with my writing. He belongs here with us."

The woman blinks, taken aback by my response.

"Now, did you want to buy that book, or were you just using it as an excuse to gossip about my family?"

Her face flushes. "I—I think I'll just browse a bit more."

She hurries away, and I feel a mixture of satisfaction and anxiety. Dad would tell me to be polite to customers, but I couldn't just stand there while she talked about him like that.

I look over to where he's still helping the book club ladies, patiently answering their questions while they sneak glances at him like he's suddenly become an exotic species. He catches my eye and gives me a small smile, and I realize with absolute certainty that I would do anything to protect that smile.

* * *

"I'm not saying we hide," Dad says, his voice tight with frustration. "I'm just saying we don't need to announce it to the entire town."

I freeze outside the kitchen door, grocery bag clutched in my hand. Dad and Thomas are arguing—I've never heard them argue before.

"No one's announcing anything," Thomas replies. "But I'm not going back in the closet, Oliver. Not even a little bit."

"That's not what I'm asking."

"Then what are you asking? Because it sounds like you want me to stop coming to the store, stop being seen with you in public."

"I'm asking for some discretion while Lily adjusts! She's getting comments at school, Thomas."

My stomach drops. I didn't want him to worry about that.

"And hiding will make it better?" Thomas sounds incredulous. "Teaching her that there's something shameful about our relation-ship?"

"That's not fair."

"No, what's not fair is asking me to pretend we're just friends in public. I did that for years, Oliver. Years of writing about you, dreaming about you, while keeping it all hidden. I can't do it again."

There's silence, and I hold my breath.

"I'm not ashamed of us," Dad finally says, his voice softer now. "I'm trying to protect Lily."

"I know." Thomas sighs. "But maybe the best protection is showing her how to face this head-on. How to be proud of who she is and who her family is."

I decide it's time to make my presence known. I push open the door, pretending I haven't heard anything.

"Got the cinnamon," I announce, holding up the grocery bag.

They both turn, looking slightly guilty.

"Thanks, Lily," Dad says. "We were just discussing the science fair tomorrow."

I set the bag on the counter. "You mean you were discussing whether Thomas should come or not."

They exchange looks.

"I heard you arguing," I admit. "And I want Thomas to come."

"Lily, some of the kids at school—"

"Are jerks," I finish for him. "And they'll be jerks whether Thomas comes or not. At least if he's there, I'll have both of you to support me."

Thomas looks at Dad with a raised eyebrow. "Smart kid, I definitely know where she didn't get that from."

Dad runs a hand through his hair, sighing. "Are you sure, Lily? People will talk."

"Let them," I say with more confidence than I feel. "My project is about interstellar communication. Who better to have there than a famous sci-fi author?"

Thomas shakes his head ruefully. "I keep getting the feeling that you're only supportive of your dad and me being together so you can use my sci-fi credentials."

"Can't it be both?" I reply, grinning unrepentantly.

* * *

The science fair is packed with students, parents, and teachers milling around the gymnasium. My project stands on a table near the centre—"Messaging the Stars: Theoretical Methods for Interstellar Communication." I've included references to some of the communication methods from Thomas's books, with his permission of course.

Dad and Thomas walk in together, and I notice heads turning, whispers starting. But something unexpected happens—Thomas waves to someone across the room, and a group of kids rushes over, clutching books and papers.

"It's Thomas Winters!" one boy exclaims. "Can you sign my book?"

Suddenly, Thomas is surrounded by fans—students and parents alike—all eager to meet him. Dad stands slightly to the side, watching with a bemused expression as Thomas charms everyone.

When they finally make it to my table, Thomas beams at my display. "This is brilliant, Lily."

"Thanks." I can't help but feel proud. "I used some ideas from Navigator Chen's communication array in book three."

"I see that." He points to one of my diagrams. "You've improved on it, though. This frequency modulation is much more efficient than what I described."

Mrs. Peterson, my science teacher, approaches. "Mr. Winters, what a surprise to have you here. Are you a friend of the family?"

Before Thomas can answer, Dad steps forward and takes Thomas's hand. "Thomas is my partner," he says clearly.

Mrs. Peterson doesn't miss a beat. "How wonderful! No wonder Lily has such creative scientific theories. She has two brilliant minds at home."

I watch Dad's shoulders relax slightly as Mrs. Peterson engages Thomas in a conversation about science fiction's influence on real scientific advancement. Across the gym, I notice Jake Collins watching us, but when he sees me looking, he quickly turns away.

"Your project is amazing, Lily," Dad says, examining my display. "Your mom would be so proud."

"I think she would be proud of all of us," I reply quietly.

Dad's eyes shine with unshed tears as he pulls me into a hug.

* * *

I flip the "Closed for Private Event" sign to face outward, take a deep breath, and step back to survey our work. Harbour Books has transformed. Rainbow streamers twist between bookshelves. Tables covered in literature about LGBTQ+ history line the walls. Dad's special-ordered Pride flag hangs behind the register, its colours bright against the exposed brick.

"What do you think?" Dad asks, adjusting a stack of "Love is Love" buttons.

"It's perfect." I straighten a poster announcing tonight's fundraiser for Harbour Point Pride. "Thomas would freak if he could see this."

Dad smiles. "He'll be back from his publisher meeting tomorrow. Just in time to hear how it went."

When Dad first proposed hosting this fundraiser, I worried. Not because I didn't support it—I was the one who showed him the Harbour Point Pride website after all—but because of how people might react. But Dad surprised me.

"I'm done hiding, Lily," he'd said, determination hardening his voice. "If Harbour Books can't be a place that celebrates all kinds of love, then what's the point?"

The doorbell chimes, interrupting my thoughts.

"We're not open yet—" Dad starts, then breaks into a grin. "Ellie! And the whole GSA crew!"

My best friend leads a parade of teenagers wearing rainbow pins. Behind them, Ms. Peterson carries a tray of cupcakes frosted in Pride colours.

"We came early to help," Ellie announces. "The Alliance voted unanimously to support Harbour Books."

Dad's eyes grow suspiciously bright. "That means a lot."

More people arrive—the sci-fi book club from Millfield, the mystery lovers from Oakridge, even the poetry society from Westbrook. Soon the store hums with activity.

Mrs. Henderson appears in the doorway, clutching her purse. She hasn't entered Harbour Books since Dad and Thomas became public knowledge.

"Oliver," she says stiffly. "I wanted to see what all the fuss was about."

Dad straightens his shoulders. "We're raising money for LGBTQ+ youth programs."

She surveys the room, lips pursed. "Well. I suppose books should be for everyone."

It's not exactly a ringing endorsement, but she drops a twenty in the donation jar before leaving.

Not everyone is so civil. Reverend Mackey and three church members stand across the street with "Family Values" signs. A few customers see them and turn away.

But for every person who walks past, three more come in. By seven o'clock, Harbour Books overflows with supporters.

"Your dad's pretty brave," Ellie says, helping me refill the refreshment table.

I watch Dad laughing with the Millfield book club, relaxed in a way I haven't seen in years.

"Yeah," I say. "He really is."

* * *

Late that night, I sit at my desk, typing furiously on my laptop. My story about Mira and the memory stars is flowing like never before. In tonight's scene, Mira stands up to a group of planetary officials who want to shut down her communication with the stars because they fear what's different.

"The stars don't just hold memories," Mira told them, her voice steady despite her racing heart. "They hold possibilities. Different ways of being. Different kinds of love. Why are you so afraid of that?"

I pause, fingers hovering over the keyboard. Today at the science fair, when Dad took Thomas's hand and called him his partner, something shifted. Not just for them, but for me too. It was like watching Captain Elian and Navigator Chen finally admit their feelings after four books of tension.

I continue typing:

The oldest official stepped forward. "It's not about fear. It's about protection."

"Protection from what?" Mira challenged. "From knowing that the universe is bigger and more beautiful than we imagined? That's not protection. That's prison."

I think about Jake Collins and Mrs. Hoffman and all the whispers. Then I think about Thomas signing books for excited kids, about Mrs. Peterson's easy acceptance, about Dad's face when he finally stopped hiding.

My story isn't just about stars anymore. It's about finding your voice. Standing your ground. Building a family that might look different from others but shines just as bright.

I type the last lines of the chapter:

The stars above Mira pulsed with light, as if applauding her courage. She didn't need everyone to understand. She just needed to be true to the constellation of her own heart.

Chapter 13

Thomas

The words flow from my fingers like water breaking through a dam. For weeks now, I've been writing with an ease I haven't felt in years—maybe ever. The final Captain Elian novel is taking shape, the story unfolding with an authenticity that had been missing when I tried forcing it.

My laptop hums as I type furiously, barely keeping pace with the thoughts racing through my mind. The cottage's living room has become my sanctuary, with papers and notes scattered across every surface. The windows frame the ocean beyond, its rhythmic presence a constant companion to my writing process.

I check the word count: thirteen thousand words today alone. The scene I've just finished shows Navigator Chen finally confronting Captain Elian about why she left their home planet fifteen years ago. The parallels to my own life with Oliver aren't subtle, but they're honest in a way my writing hasn't been before.

A knock at the door pulls me from the depths of space.

"It's open," I call, saving my document with a quick keystroke.

Lily appears, clutching her notebook to her chest, her expression a mixture of frustration and determination.

"Hey, Thomas. Are you busy?"

"Never too busy for you." I close my laptop and clear a space on the couch. "What's up?"

She sits beside me, opening her notebook to reveal pages filled with her neat handwriting, marred by crossouts and margin notes.

"I'm stuck. Like, really stuck." She points to a paragraph halfway down the page. "Mira is supposed to find this special star that holds her mother's memories, but everything I write feels..." She scrunches her nose. "Fake."

I take the notebook, scanning the section she's struggling with. Her story has grown impressively over the past few weeks—a young girl who discovers stars contain memories from different civilizations, including possibly her deceased mother.

"This reminds me of where I was with my book a month ago." I hand the notebook back. "Want to know what helped me break through?"

She nods eagerly, tucking a strand of hair behind her ear.

"I stopped trying to write what I thought the story should be and started writing what it needed to be." I reach for my own notebook. "Here, let me show you something."

I flip through pages of scribbled notes until I find what I'm looking for—my early attempts at the final Captain Elian book.

"See this?" I point to a heavily crossed-out section. "This was me forcing Captain Elian to stay away from Navigator Chen because I thought that's what made dramatic sense. But it wasn't true to who she is."

Lily studies the page. "So what did you do?"

"I asked myself what I would do if I were in her position. What would make me finally return to someone I'd never stopped loving?"

Her eyes widen with understanding. "So for Mira, I need to think about what would make her brave enough to reach for her mom's memories, even though it might hurt."

"Exactly. What would you do if you could reach for memories of someone you've lost?"

Lily grows quiet, her fingers tracing the edge of her notebook. "I'd want to know if she was proud of me."

The simplicity and honesty of her answer catches in my chest.

"That's it, Lily. That's your scene. Mira doesn't just want any memory—she wants to know if her mother was proud of her. That's what drives her to that particular star."

Her face lights up. "Yes! And maybe she's afraid of what she'll find, but she goes anyway because..."

"Because knowing is better than wondering," I finish.

She's already scribbling in her notebook, ideas flowing. I watch her write, recognizing the same creative fire that's been fueling my own work.

"You know what helped me too?" I add. "Having a specific place to write. Somewhere that feels like it belongs to the story."

"Dad just reads at the kitchen table," she says, not looking up from her writing.

I smile. "Well, maybe we can change that."

* * *

The next day, I arrive at Harbour Books with coffee for Oliver and hot chocolate for Lily. The morning rush has just subsided, and I find Oliver rearranging books on a display near the front window.

"Delivery for the most handsome bookseller in town," I announce, holding up the drinks.

Oliver's face softens at the sight of me. "You're spoiling me."

"That's the plan." I hand him his coffee, stealing a quick kiss. "Where's Lily?"

"Stockroom. She's organizing the new shipment of sci-fi novels."

I follow him to the counter, where he sets down his drink and checks something on the computer.

"I had an idea I wanted to run by you," I say, leaning against the counter. "Lily came to me yesterday stuck on her story."

Oliver looks up, suddenly concerned. "Is she okay?"

"More than okay. She's working through the same creative process professional writers do. But it got me thinking—what if we created a dedicated writing space here at the store? A little nook where she could work on her stories, and maybe where I could work sometimes too."

Oliver's expression shifts from surprise to consideration. "Like a writer's corner?"

"Exactly. It would give her a space that feels special, separate from homework or other obligations. And selfishly, it would give me an excuse to spend more time here with you both."

He studies my face, a smile playing at the corners of his mouth. "You're serious about this."

"I am. Writing changed my life, Oliver. And seeing how it's lighting Lily up..." I shrug. "I just want to nurture that."

He's quiet for a moment, then nods decisively. "The alcove by the science fiction section. It gets great natural light, and it's tucked away enough to feel private."

My heart swells at how quickly he embraces the idea. "It would be perfect."

"I've been meaning to rearrange that section anyway." He takes a sip of his coffee, eyes already calculating the work involved. "We could move the display shelves, bring in a desk, maybe a comfortable chair..."

"Dad?" Lily emerges from the stockroom, clipboard in hand. "Oh, hi Thomas!"

"Your timing is perfect," Oliver says. "Thomas had an idea I think you'll like."

* * *

Three days later, the writing nook is complete. Oliver has transformed the alcove into a cozy retreat, with a vintage writing desk facing the window, a comfortable chair, and floating shelves holding reference books and writing supplies. A small sign hangs above it: "Worlds in Progress."

Lily stands in the centre of it, turning slowly to take in every detail. "It's perfect."

Oliver places a hand on her shoulder. "The desk was your grandfather's. I found it in the attic."

She runs her fingers over the smooth wood surface. "Can I really work here whenever I want?"

"That's the idea," I say. "A dedicated space for Harbour Books' resident writers."

"Writers. Plural." She looks up at me. "You'll use it too?"

"If that's okay with you. We can work out a schedule."

She shakes her head. "No schedule. I want to see you write. I want to learn how you do it."

Oliver catches my eye over her head, his expression soft with gratitude.

"Deal," I say. "In fact, how about we christen it right now? I brought something for both of you."

I reach into my messenger bag and pull out two leather-bound journals—one dark blue, one deep purple.

"For your works in progress," I explain, handing the purple one to Lily and the blue one to Oliver. "And before you protest," I add, seeing Oliver's surprise, "this one is for the poetry I know you still write when you think no one's looking."

His cheeks flush. "How did you—"

"I found your notebook when I was helping organize the office last week," Lily admits. "Sorry, Dad."

Oliver looks between us, caught between embarrassment and amusement. "I see I'm outnumbered."

"Completely," I confirm. "Now, what do you say we start a tradition? Every evening, after the store closes, we share what we've written that day."

Lily clutches her journal to her chest. "Like a writer's circle?"

"Exactly like that."

Oliver's hand finds mine, squeezing gently. "I think that sounds wonderful."

* * *

The evening reading sessions quickly become my favourite part of each day. After Harbour Books closes, we gather in the writing nook with cups of tea and take turns reading our day's work.

Lily's story grows richer with each session. She's woven elements of her own experiences into her fictional world—a mother who exists among the stars, a father who runs a library of cosmic knowledge, and a mysterious visitor who helps the young protagonist understand her connection to the universe.

"Mira stands at the observatory window," Lily reads from her journal, her voice gaining confidence with each word. "The star her father pointed out pulses with a light that seems to call only to her. 'What if I reach for it and find nothing?' she whispers. The librarian places a hand on her shoulder. 'What if you reach for it and find everything?'"

When she finishes the passage, Oliver and I exchange glances, both recognizing the parallels to our own story.

"That's beautiful, Lily," Oliver says, his voice thick with emotion.

"Really beautiful," I agree. "The way you've captured Mira's fear and hope at the same time—that's not easy to do."

She beams at the praise. "Your turn, Thomas."

I open my laptop where I've been working on the climactic scene of my novel. "Captain Elian stands at the navigation console, her hand hovering over the controls. The coordinates for Vega are already entered, the ship ready to make the jump. 'What if I go back and everything's changed?' she asks. Navigator Chen steps forward, his presence steady as always. 'What if you go back and find that some things never change at all?'"

Oliver's eyes meet mine over the top of my screen, and I see in them the same mixture of wonder and recognition that I feel whenever I write these characters now.

"Your turn, Dad," Lily prompts.

Oliver hesitates, then opens his blue journal. "It's just a short poem."

"Those are the best kind," I encourage.

He clears his throat. "'The stars align differently now / Than when we were young / But still guide us home / To the same Harbour.'"

The simplicity and truth of his words leave me speechless. Lily claps her hands together.

"Dad! That's so good!"

Oliver shrugs, but I can see the pleasure in his eyes at our reaction. "Just something I was thinking about while watching you two work today."

I reach across the desk to take his hand. "It's perfect."

* * *

Weeks pass in this new rhythm. I split my time between the cottage and Harbour Books, writing wherever inspiration strikes. My manuscript grows steadily, the story reaching toward its natural conclusion with an inevitability that feels right.

One afternoon, as rain patters against the bookstore windows, I look up from my laptop to find Lily watching me work.

"How do you know when you're near the end?" she asks.

I consider her question carefully. "The story starts to pull itself together. All the threads you've been weaving suddenly form a pattern you couldn't see before."

She nods thoughtfully. "I think I'm getting close with Mira's story."

"Me too," I admit. "With Captain Elian."

The realization hits me fully as I say it aloud. After months of struggling, after fifteen years of writing this series, I'm finally approaching the end. Captain Elian and Navigator Chen's journey is coming full circle, just as mine and Oliver's has.

"Does that make you sad?" Lily asks, perceptive as always.

"A little," I admit. "These characters have been with me for so long. But it also feels right. They deserve their ending."

"A happy one?"

I smile. "The kind of happy that comes after you've earned it. After you've learned what matters most."

Oliver appears from between the bookshelves, catching the tail end of our conversation. "Talking about endings?"

"Beginnings disguised as endings," I correct, watching him move toward us.

He rests his hand on my shoulder, and I reach up to cover it with my own. "The best kind," he says softly.

Lily looks between us, satisfaction written across her face. "I think I know how to finish Mira's story now."

"How?" I ask.

She gathers her notebook and stands. "She doesn't just find her mother's memories in the stars. She finds a way to create new ones that honour the old ones."

As she heads to the writing desk to work on her ending, Oliver takes the seat she vacated.

"She picked that up from you, you know," he says quietly. "That sudden ability to see the heart of things."

I shake my head. "That's one hundred percent all you. You've always seen me more clearly than I see myself."

He leans forward, pressing his forehead against mine for a moment. "How close are you really? To finishing?"

"Two, maybe three more chapters. For the first time, I can see exactly how it ends."

"And how does it end?" His voice is barely above a whisper.

I smile, thinking of Captain Elian and Navigator Chen, of the journey that brought them—and us—to this point.

"They find their way back to each other," I tell him. "And discover that home was never a place at all."

Chapter 14

Thomas

I wake to the sound of Oliver's steady breathing beside me, his arm draped across my chest. Sunlight filters through unfamiliar curtains—blue with tiny sailboats that Lily picked out years ago, Oliver told me. This marks the fourth morning this week I've woken in Oliver's bed instead of at the cottage. Not that I'm complaining, far from it really.

The digital clock on his nightstand reads 6:38. Early, but not too early. I ease myself from under Oliver's arm, smiling when he mumbles something incoherent and burrows deeper into the pillow. The hardwood floor is cool beneath my feet as I pad to the kitchen.

By now, I know where everything is—coffee filters in the drawer next to the sink, Oliver's favourite mug (a faded Harbour Books logo) on the second shelf, the temperamental coffee maker that needs an extra push on the power button. I move through the morning ritual that's becoming mine too.

"You're still here." Lily appears in the doorway, her hair a mess of tangles, wearing Star Wars pyjamas.

"I am," I confirm, pouring water into the coffee maker. "Is that okay?"

She yawns dramatically. "As long as you make enough coffee for Dad.

He's grumpy without it."

"Noted." I reach for another mug. "Hot chocolate for you?"

"Yes, please." She slides onto a stool at the kitchen island, watching me navigate her kitchen with growing familiarity. "You know where everything is now."

"Getting there." I set the milk to warm. "Your dad's a creature of habit. Makes it easier to learn."

She props her chin on her hands. "Mom used to say that too."

The mention of Sarah doesn't sting the way it might have weeks ago. Instead, it feels like an acknowledgement of the space we're all navigating together.

"Thomas?" Her voice turns serious. "Would you come with me somewhere today? Just us?"

I pour her hot chocolate into a mug shaped like R2-D2. "Sure. Where to?"

"I want to visit Mom." She accepts the mug, wrapping her hands around it. "Dad goes too much. Makes him sad. But I haven't been in a while, and I want to tell her about my story."

The request catches me off guard. "Are you sure you want me there? It seems private."

"I'm sure." Her eyes, so like Oliver's, hold mine steadily. "She would have liked you. Dad said so."

* * *

The cemetery sits on a gentle hill overlooking the Harbour. Lily leads the way confidently through rows of headstones, clutching a small bouquet of wildflowers we picked on the way. I follow a few steps behind, giving her space while staying close.

Sarah's grave is simple—a polished stone with her name, dates, and the inscription "Beloved mother, wife, and friend. Her light guides us still."

Lily kneels to arrange the flowers in the small vase embedded in the ground. I hang back, uncertain of my place here.

"It's okay," she says without looking up. "You can come closer."

I step forward, standing beside her. The breeze carries the scent of salt from the Harbour below.

"Hi, Mom," Lily says conversationally. "I brought Thomas with me today. He's Dad's... well, you know. The one from the books. He came back and now he's part of the family."

We sit in silence for a moment, the distant sound of waves breaking against the shore below us.

"I'm writing a story now," she tells the headstone. "About a girl named Mira who talks to stars. Thomas is helping me. He says I have talent."

"She does," I confirm, feeling strangely like Sarah might actually be listening. "Real talent."

Lily reaches out suddenly, taking my hand. The gesture is so unexpected that I almost pull away, but her grip is firm.

"Mom always said stories help us understand things we can't say out loud." She looks at me, her eyes shining with unshed tears. "Is that why you write about families in your books? To understand?"

The question pierces me. "I suppose I do. Captain Elian's crew becomes her family. They choose each other."

"Like we're choosing each other," Lily says simply.

I squeeze her hand, unable to speak past the lump in my throat.

"I think Mom would be happy," she continues, turning back to the headstone. "That we're not alone anymore. That's what she worried about most, Dad said. That we'd be alone."

We stay until the breeze turns chilly, Lily occasionally speaking to her mother about school, her story, ordinary things. I remain silent, honoured to witness this communion between daughter and mother.

As we walk back to the car, Lily looks up at me. "In your books, how do you know what makes a real family?"

I consider this carefully. "I think... a real family are the people who see you clearly and love you anyway. Who choose to stay even when it's difficult."

She nods, processing this. "That's what I thought too."

* * *

"Carry the two," I explain, pointing at Lily's math homework spread across the kitchen table. "Then multiply by the coefficient."

She groans, dropping her head dramatically onto her notebook. "Why do I need algebra if I'm going to be a writer?"

"Because writers need to understand patterns," I tell her, sliding her pencil back into her hand. "Math is just another language."

"A terrible one," she mutters, but starts working through the problem again.

From the doorway, Oliver watches us, a small smile playing at his lips. I catch his eye and return the smile, this quiet moment of domesticity still new enough to feel miraculous.

"Need help?" he asks, entering with a basket of laundry balanced on his hip.

"We've got it," I assure him. "Though your daughter believes algebra is a form of torture specifically designed for her."

"It is!" Lily insists, but she's smiling now.

Oliver sets the laundry basket on the counter and begins folding. Without thinking, I rise to help him, taking shirts from the pile and folding them the way I've noticed he prefers—sleeves first, then sides.

"You don't have to—" he begins.

"I know," I interrupt gently. "I want to."

We work side by side, folding clothes, while Lily tackles her algebra.

The mundane task feels oddly significant—this sharing of household duties, this integration into their rhythms.

"Dad, can we go to North Beach this weekend?" Lily asks suddenly. "The weather's supposed to be perfect."

Oliver glances at me. "Thomas might have writing to do."

"Actually," I say, "a beach day sounds perfect. I could use some sunshine."

Lily beams. "We can bring the kite! And sandwiches! And Thomas can read us what he wrote this week!"

"Sounds like a plan," Oliver agrees, his eyes warm as they meet mine over a pile of folded towels.

* * *

North Beach stretches empty before us, the tourist season long over. Oliver spreads a blanket while Lily immediately runs toward the water's edge, her kite trailing behind her.

"Not too close to the water!" Oliver calls after her.

"I know, Dad!" she shouts back, the wind carrying her voice.

I set down our picnic basket and cooler. "She's in her element out here."

"Always has been," Oliver confirms, watching his daughter with fond eyes. "Sarah used to say she was born with salt water in her veins."

I unpack sandwiches and thermoses of hot chocolate. "Thank you for including me today."

Oliver looks at me, surprise evident on his face. "Of course. You're part of—" He stops, uncertain.

"Part of?" I prompt gently.

"This," he gestures vaguely. "Us."

The simple word contains multitudes. Us. A concept I've written about for years but never truly experienced until now.

"Dad! Thomas! Come fly the kite with me!" Lily waves frantically from the shoreline.

We join her, taking turns with the kite string, laughing when the wind suddenly drops and the kite plummets. Oliver teaches me the trick of running backward to create lift, his hands guiding mine on the string. Lily documents everything with her phone, directing us into poses, capturing moments.

"Family photo!" she declares, propping her phone against the picnic basket and setting the timer. She runs back to us, positioning herself between Oliver and me.

"Ready?" she asks as the timer counts down.

Oliver's arm slips around my waist, natural and right. I drape mine across his shoulders, my other hand resting lightly on Lily's shoulder. The camera flashes.

Later, as we eat sandwiches on the blanket, Lily pulls out her notebook. "I worked on a new scene last night. Can I read it to you guys?"

"Absolutely," I encourage, settling back on my elbows.

She clears her throat dramatically. "'Mira watched as the star's light formed shapes in her room—not just random patterns, but images of people. Her mother was there, smiling, but so were new faces. The star captain who'd helped her understand the messages. The neighbors who brought dinner every Tuesday. Her father's friend who taught her about constellations.'"

She pauses, looking up at us. "'The star seemed to pulse with understanding. 'Family isn't just who you're born to,' it whispered. 'It's also who you choose to love along the way.'"

Oliver's hand finds mine on the blanket between us, squeezing gently.

"That's beautiful, Lily," I tell her honestly. "You've captured something really important there."

She beams, closing her notebook. "It's the turning point for Mira. When she realizes she doesn't have to choose between honouring her mom's memory and building something new."

Her words hang in the air between us, profound in their simplicity. I look at Oliver, whose eyes have grown suspiciously bright.

* * *

The evening finds us back at Oliver's house, Lily already in bed after an exhausting day at the beach. Oliver and I sit on the back porch, watching stars appear one by one above the Harbour.

"Lily showed me the photo from today," Oliver says quietly, passing me his phone.

The image shows the three of us on the beach—windblown, sandy, and undeniably happy. Something about seeing it makes my throat tighten.

"We look like a family," I say, the words barely audible.

Oliver takes a deep breath. "That's what scares me sometimes. How easily you fit with us. How right it feels." He stares out at the darkening Harbour. "Then I feel guilty. Like I'm replacing Sarah."

I hand back his phone. "You're not replacing anyone, Oliver. Sarah will always be Lily's mother. Always be part of who you both are."

"I know that logically," he admits. "But emotions aren't logical."

"No," I agree. "They're not."

"Sarah told me something once, near the end." His voice is soft, reflective. "She said, 'When you find love again, don't waste time feeling guilty. Just make sure it's the real thing.'"

I take his hand, intertwining our fingers. "And is it? The real thing?"

He turns to me, his eyes reflecting starlight. "You know it is. It always was."

"Then honour her by being happy," I tell him. "By letting Lily see what real love looks like. By living fully."

He leans into me, his head resting against my shoulder. "When did you get so wise?"

"I'm a writer," I remind him. "I just pretend to understand the human heart."

His laugh vibrates against me. "You do more than pretend."

We sit in companionable silence, watching the stars emerge fully. Tomorrow, I'll return to the cottage to pack some of my things. The lease runs another month, but increasingly, my life is here, in this house, with these people.

"Stay tonight," Oliver says, as if reading my thoughts. "And tomorrow. And the day after."

"I was thinking of bringing some of my books over," I venture. "And maybe my winter clothes. The cottage is starting to get drafty now that the nights are cooler."

He sits up, looking at me. "Are you asking to move in?"

"Not exactly. Not yet." I choose my words carefully. "But maybe... a gradual transition? Some of my things here, some there, until we figure out what makes sense."

His smile is slow and sure. "I'd like that."

Tomorrow, I'll pack books and clothes, my favourite coffee mug and the typewriter I keep for sentimental reasons. I'll bring them here, to this house that's becoming home, to these people who are becoming family.

But tonight, I simply lean into Oliver under the stars, feeling the pieces of my life finally falling into place.

The night air grows cooler as we sit together under the stars. Oliver shivers slightly against me, and I pull him closer, feeling a familiar heat build between us.

"Should we go inside?" I whisper against his ear, my body already responding to his proximity, anticipating what's to come. I breathe in the intoxicating scent of salt and sunshine from our day at the beach.

He nods, rising slowly from the porch swing. Our hands remain linked as we move through the darkened house, careful not to make noise that might wake Lily. The floorboards creak softly beneath our feet as Oliver's hand slides possessively to the small of my back, guiding me forward.

In Oliver's bedroom—our bedroom, increasingly—moonlight spills through the half-open curtains, casting everything in silver and shadow. Oliver closes the door behind us with a soft click, immediately pressing me against it, his mouth finding mine with hungry precision.

"I've been wanting you all day," he murmurs against my lips, his thigh pressing between my legs, creating delicious friction against my hardening cock. "Watching you play with Lily in the waves, helping her build that ridiculous sandcastle..."

"What?" I ask, already breathless as his hands slip beneath my shirt, thumbs brushing over my nipples.

"Just thinking about how different this is from that first night at your cottage," he says, his fingers finding the buttons of my shirt with practiced ease, exposing my chest inch by tantalizing inch. "When everything felt impossible and inevitable at the same time."

I catch his hands, bringing them to my lips. "And now?"

His eyes darken with desire. "Now it just feels right." His gaze holds mine, steady and certain as his hands move to my waistband. "Like we're exactly where we're supposed to be."

Since that first desperate reunion at the cottage, we've learned each other again—mapped the changes in our bodies, discovered new sensitivities, reawakened old ones. I've discovered how much I love surrendering to Oliver, how his confidence in bed makes me feel both vulnerable and completely safe.

He draws me toward the bed, his hands working my jeans down my hips. "I love watching you with Lily," he says, his voice husky with desire. "The way you listen to her ideas, how seriously you take her writing."

I step out of my jeans, helping Oliver out of his shirt. "I love becoming part of your lives," I confess, running my hands over the broad expanse of his chest, feeling the steady beat of his heart beneath my palm. "The way I fold laundry exactly how you do it. How I know Lily takes her hot chocolate with three marshmallows, not two."

His eyes soften momentarily before darkening again with need. He captures my mouth with his, our tongues sliding together in a rhythm that mimics what I want him to do to me.

We undress each other with practiced efficiency, no longer shy but still reverent. The moonlight reveals Oliver's body to me—broader and stronger than mine, the muscles in his arms defined from years of carrying boxes of books, the trail of dark hair leading down from his navel to his impressive erection.

"I never imagined this," Oliver says as he guides me to the bed, pressing me down onto my back. "Even when I hoped you'd come back someday, I never let myself imagine actually having this."

"Having what?" I ask, watching as he retrieves the lube from the nightstand drawer.

His hand traces my face with tender precision. "Ordinary moments. Helping Lily with homework. Watching you make coffee in the morning." His voice catches as he settles between my thighs. "Planning beach days together. A future."

Something shifts between us—not the desperate reunion of that first night, nor the eager rediscovery of the nights that followed. This is something new, something profound in its simplicity, even as our bodies demand satisfaction.

"I'm not just coming back to what we had," I tell him, spreading my legs wider in invitation. "I'm coming home to what we can be."

Oliver's eyes shine in the darkness as he slicks his fingers. "Show me."

The first breach of his finger makes me gasp, my body arching off the bed. Oliver works me open with patient expertise, adding a second finger, then a third, each movement calculated to brush against that bundle of nerves that makes stars explode behind my eyelids.

"Please, Oliver," I finally beg, my voice a ragged whisper. "I need you inside me."

He positions himself between my thighs, the blunt head of his cock nudging against my prepared entrance. "Look at me," he commands softly. "I want to see your eyes when I fill you."

Our gazes lock as he pushes forward, the exquisite stretch of him entering me drawing a low moan from my throat. Oliver's face is a study in concentration and pleasure as he sinks into me inch by delicious inch. When he's fully seated within me, we both pause, adjusting to the overwhelming sensation of completeness.

Unlike our first night together when we reclaimed each other with almost desperate intensity, tonight Oliver establishes a deliberate, unhurried pace. Each thrust is measured, angled to hit that spot inside me that makes my vision blur. I wrap my legs around his waist, drawing him deeper, my hands clutching at his shoulders.

"You feel incredible," Oliver whispers, his breath hot against my ear. "So tight around me. Like you were made for this—for me."

His words send shivers down my spine, heightening every sensation. My neglected cock throbs between us, leaking against my stomach. As if reading my mind, Oliver wraps his hand around it, stroking in counterpoint to his thrusts.

"I never stopped loving you," he confesses, the words punctuated by the rhythmic slap of skin against skin. "Even when I tried."

"I wrote my way back to you," I tell him, feeling my climax building at the base of my spine. "Every word, every book—just trying to find my way home."

The dual sensation of Oliver inside me and his hand working my cock pushes me over the edge. I come with his name on my lips, my release painting hot stripes across my chest and stomach. The sight of me completely undone pushes Oliver to his limit, and he drives into me one final time, emptying himself deep inside me, marking me as his in the most primal way.

He collapses beside me, both of us breathing heavily. Oliver trails his fingers through the mess on my stomach, bringing them to his lips to taste me. I watch with hooded eyes, my body still tingling with aftershocks.

"When you bring your things tomorrow," Oliver says eventually, his voice soft but certain, "bring everything."

I tilt my face to his, searching his eyes. "Everything?"

"No more gradual transition," he says, his hand possessively resting on my thigh. "No more half measures. Move in, Thomas. Be here when I wake up every morning. Help Lily with her homework. Write your books in the writing nook we built for you and Lily."

My heart swells at his words and I kiss him deeply. "Yes," I whisper against his lips. "To all of it. Yes."

Oliver pulls me against his chest, his arms wrapped protectively around me. I feel his seed slowly leaking from me, a physical reminder of our connection. His breathing gradually slows toward sleep, but I remain awake, holding this moment close—not as a culmination but as a beginning. After fifteen years of writing stories about the stars, I've finally found my place on Earth, right here in this bed, in this house, with these people who are becoming my family.

Tomorrow, I'll bring everything. Not just my possessions, but all of me—ready to write not just Captain Elian's final chapter, but the next chapter of our own story.

Chapter 15

Thomas

The cursor blinks on my screen like a patient heartbeat, waiting for the next words. I've been staring at it for ten minutes, not because I'm stuck, but because I'm savouring this moment. After months of struggling, I'm writing the final chapters of Captain Elian's journey.

"Is it weird that I can hear you thinking?" Lily asks from the armchair across the room.

I glance up to find her curled in what has become her designated spot in my—our—writing nook at Harbour Books. The wall behind us displays framed covers of my books alongside Lily's science fair certificates.

"Just gathering my thoughts," I tell her. "How's Mira doing today?"

Lily taps her pencil against her notebook. "She's finally finding her mom's memories in the star clusters. I'm trying to make it scientific but also, you know, magical."

"The best science fiction lives in that perfect space between the two."

She nods seriously, then returns to her writing. I watch her for a moment, this remarkable girl who has somehow become part of my life. She's so much like Oliver—thoughtful, determined, with that same little crease between her eyebrows when she concentrates.

I turn back to my manuscript. On screen, Captain Elian stands at the helm of her ship, the final approach to Vega Prime before her. Navigator Chen waits planetside, fifteen years older but still wearing the stars in his eyes. My fingers hover over the keyboard, then begin to move with certainty.

Captain Elian had travelled the known universe, mapped the farthest reaches of the Proxima Quadrant, and negotiated peace between warring civilizations. Yet nothing had prepared her for the simple, terrifying act of coming home.

For two hours, we write in companionable silence, interrupted only by the occasional customer wandering back to browse the science fiction section. Oliver appears periodically with tea for me, hot chocolate for Lily, and quiet pride in his eyes as he watches us work.

"Thomas?" Lily's voice pulls me from deep within the story. "Can I read you something?"

"Always."

She clears her throat. "Mira pressed her palm against the observatory glass, feeling the cold seep into her skin. The star cluster pulsed in patterns that reminded her of her mother's heartbeat, the one she used to fall asleep against as a child. 'I know you're there,' she whispered, 'and I know you can hear me.'"

My chest tightens. "That's beautiful, Lily."

"Do you think it's too much? Too... I don't know, sappy?"

"The best stories come from emotional truth," I tell her. "Never be afraid of writing from your heart."

She considers this, then nods and returns to her notebook with renewed purpose. I watch her for another moment before diving back into my own world, where Captain Elian is finally reuniting with Navigator Chen after fifteen years apart.

"You kept them all," Elian said, running her fingers along the shelf of mission logs she'd sent back from the furthest reaches of space.

Chen's smile held fifteen years of patience. "Every transmission. Every star chart. Every word you ever sent home."

"I never thought you'd wait."

"I never thought you'd return," he countered. "Yet here we are."

The words flow easily now, the culmination of a journey I started fifteen years ago when I first left Harbour Point—and Oliver—behind. In my fiction, I'm giving us the reunion we deserved, the one we're finally getting in real life. As I type the final scene, I realize I'm crying, quiet tears tracking down my cheeks.

"Dad says it's time for dinner," Lily announces, suddenly beside me. She notices my tears and her eyes widen. "Are you okay?"

I wipe my face, embarrassed but not ashamed. "I just finished."

Her face lights up. "The whole book? The very end?"

"The very end."

She bounces on her toes. "Can I read it? Please?"

"Your dad gets first read," I tell her. "Author's honour."

"But I'm second, right?"

I laugh, saving the document and closing my laptop. "You're definitely second."

* * *

Oliver's hands tremble slightly as he turns the final page of the manuscript. We're sitting on the deck of what is now our home, the evening air cool around us. Lily is at a friend's house for the night, giving Oliver space to read the conclusion of Captain Elian's journey without interruption.

I've been watching him read for the past three hours, studying every micro-expression that crosses his face—the small smiles, the occasional tears, the way he sometimes pauses to look out at the ocean as if gathering himself before continuing.

Now he closes the manuscript and sets it carefully on the table between us. His eyes, when they meet mine, are bright with unshed tears.

"That's us," he says simply.

I nod, unable to speak past the lump in my throat.

"You wrote us the ending we should have had fifteen years ago."

"I wrote us the ending we're having now," I correct him. "Just in space, with more laser battles."

He laughs, the sound breaking through his emotion. "I particularly enjoyed Navigator Chen saving the day with his 'unconventional orbital calculations.'"

"Well, you always were better at math than me."

Oliver reaches across the table and takes my hand. "When you left, I never imagined you were carrying me with you like this. That I was living in your imagination all these years, travelling the stars."

"You were always with me," I tell him. "In every word I wrote."

He stands, pulling me to my feet and into his arms. "Thank you for bringing Navigator Chen home."

I hold him tightly, breathing in the scent of him—books and coffee and home. "Thank you for waiting for Captain Elian."

Later, in bed, Oliver traces patterns on my chest as if mapping constellations. "Will your readers know?" he asks. "That it's us?"

"Some might suspect. Vera certainly will." I pause, thinking of my editor. "I'm sending it to her tomorrow."

"Are you nervous?"

"A little. It's different from the others. More personal."

"It's better than the others," Oliver says with certainty. "It feels... real."

I kiss the top of his head. "That's because it is."

* * *

178

"You're pacing," Lily observes from her perch on the counter. "It's making me dizzy."

I stop in the middle of the kitchen, phone clutched in my hand. "Vera said she'd call by noon."

"It's only eleven forty-five," she points out reasonably. "And Dad says you're making him nervous too."

Oliver looks up from where he's preparing lunch. "I didn't say that."

"You were thinking it," Lily and I say in unison, then grin at each other.

My phone rings, Vera's name flashing on the screen. I nearly drop it in my haste to answer.

"Hello?"

"Thomas," Vera's crisp voice comes through. "I've finished it."

I close my eyes, bracing myself. "And?"

"It's brilliant." Her voice softens. "Absolutely brilliant. The best thing you've ever written."

Relief floods through me so intensely that I have to lean against the counter. "Really?"

"The emotion in it, Thomas. The authenticity. Captain Elian has never felt more real, more human. And Chen—" She pauses. "This is personal for you, isn't it? This ending?"

I look at Oliver, who's watching me with hopeful eyes. "Yes. Very personal."

"Well, whatever—or whoever—inspired this, I'm grateful. The marketing team is going to have a field day. 'The triumphant conclusion to the bestselling series.' We'll want to fast-track publication."

We discuss details for a few more minutes before hanging up. I stand there, phone in hand, trying to process that it's done—really done. The story I've been telling for fifteen years has finally reached its conclusion.

"Well?" Oliver prompts.

"She loved it," I say, still dazed. "They're fast-tracking it for publication."

Lily squeals and launches herself at me for a hug. Oliver's smile is quieter but no less joyful as he joins us, wrapping his arms around us both.

"I knew she would," Lily says confidently. "It's the best one."

"You haven't even read it yet," I remind her.

"Dad's been reading parts to me," she admits. "The non-mushy parts."

I look at Oliver, who shrugs unapologetically. "She wore me down."

"Speaking of reading," Lily says, pulling away. "I finished my story last night. For the competition."

"The deadline's tomorrow, right?" I ask.

She nods. "I was hoping you'd read it before I submit it. Make sure it's okay."

"I'd be honoured."

Later, sitting at the kitchen table with Lily's story in my hands, I'm struck by how much she's grown as a writer in just a few weeks. Her tale of Mira and the memory-keeping stars is beautiful, poignant, and surprisingly sophisticated for a thirteen-year-old. When I finish, I find her watching me anxiously.

"Well?" she asks.

"It's wonderful," I tell her honestly. "You've created something really special here, Lily."

"Do you think it has a chance? In the competition?"

"I think it has more than a chance. But even if it doesn't win, you've written something true and beautiful. That's what matters."

She considers this, then nods. "That's what you did with Captain Elian and Navigator Chen. You wrote something true."

"I did."

"And now you're staying here with us, right? For good?"

The question catches me off guard, not because I haven't thought about it, but because of the vulnerability behind it. "Yes," I promise her. "For good."

* * *

I step onto the deck after Lily and Oliver head into town for groceries. The silence feels welcome after our emotional morning—the perfect moment to check my neglected email. My phone pings repeatedly as dozens of messages sync.

"What the—" I mutter, scrolling through an avalanche of forwarded emails from Vera.

Subject lines blur together: "Chicago Literary Festival Request," "Seattle Book Expo Keynote," "New York Comic Con Panel Invitation," "London Sci-Fi Convention."

My stomach tightens. There must be thirty event requests spanning the next eight months—readings, signings, conventions, interviews. Some as far away as Tokyo and Berlin. All forwarded with Vera's cheerful note: "The final Captain Elian book is generating HUGE interest! Let me know which of these you want to commit to!"

I sink into the deck chair, a cold weight settling in my chest. There's already eight months of travel planned. Eight months away from Harbour Point. Away from Oliver and Lily.

I just promised Lily I was staying "for good." The words echo in my mind as I continue scrolling through cities, dates, commitments.

I've done book tours before—lived out of suitcases, slept in sterile hotel rooms, signed books until my hand cramped. But that was before. Before coming home. Before finding Oliver again. Before becoming part of this family.

The final email from Vera reads: "Thomas, these are just the beginning. Once we announce the publication date, expect this to triple. This is going to be your biggest book yet!"

My finger hovers over the reply button. What do I say? That I can't go? That I won't? That I've finally found where I belong after fifteen years of wandering?

But this is my career. The culmination of everything I've worked for. The conclusion to Captain Elian's journey deserves to be celebrated, shared with the readers who've followed her for years.

I set the phone down, staring out at the ocean. The same view that inspired Navigator Chen's home planet. The same waves that have witnessed my reunion with Oliver.

How do I choose between the life I've built and the life I'm just beginning?

* * *

The table at The Lighthouse Restaurant is set for three, candles flickering in the ocean breeze coming through the open windows. Oliver insisted on taking us out to celebrate both my completed manuscript and my official move into their home.

"To new beginnings," Oliver says, raising his glass.

Lily raises her soda. "And to Thomas moving in!"

We clink glasses, and I'm struck by how right this feels—the three of us together, celebrating not just my professional milestone but our personal one as well.

Our food arrives, and the conversation shifts to lighter topics—Lily's upcoming science project, the bookstore's student reading program, my publisher's plans for a book tour after the release.

"Would you come with me?" I ask Oliver. "Both of you, I mean. For at least part of it?"

Oliver hesitates. "What about school? And the store?"

"Just for a weekend or two," I clarify. "I'd love to have you there. And I think my readers would be interested to meet the real Navigator

Chen."

"And his daughter?" Lily asks hopefully.

"Especially his daughter."

Oliver's expression is complicated—pleasure mixed with something that looks almost like fear. "We'll see," he says noncommittally.

Later, after Lily excuses herself to use the restroom, I lean toward Oliver. "What's wrong? You've seemed... distant tonight."

He stares at his half-eaten dessert. "Nothing's wrong."

"Oliver."

He sighs. "It's stupid."

"Tell me anyway."

"I keep waiting," he admits quietly. "For you to realize this isn't what you want. That you need more than a small-town bookstore owner and his teenage daughter."

The vulnerability in his voice breaks my heart. "Oliver, look at me."

He raises his eyes reluctantly.

"I spent fifteen years writing about a spaceship captain who explored the entire universe only to realize that home was the one place she truly belonged. That wasn't just fiction—it was me trying to tell myself what I really needed."

"And what do you need?" he asks, his voice barely audible.

"You," I say simply. "You and Lily and this life we're building. I'm not leaving again, Oliver. This isn't temporary for me."

He nods, but I can see the lingering doubt in his eyes—the fear born from fifteen years of absence. I know it will take time to prove to him that I'm here to stay, that I've finally found my way home. But I have all the time in the world now, and I intend to use every day to show him that our story—unlike Captain Elian's—is just beginning.

III

Part Three

Chapter 16

Thomas

I'm settling into my morning routine at Oliver's—our—house when my phone buzzes. The editor at my publisher's office flashes across the screen. My heart rate kicks up a notch. She's had the final manuscript for a week now, and her silence has been making me increasingly nervous.

"Morning, Alison," I answer, trying to sound casual.

"Thomas Winters, you magnificent bastard!" Her voice booms through the speaker with such enthusiasm that I have to hold the phone away from my ear. "I just finished it. The whole thing. In one sitting."

I exhale slowly, relief washing over me. "So... you liked it?"

"Liked it? LIKED IT?" She laughs, a sound I rarely hear from my typically composed editor. "This isn't just good, Thomas. This is transcendent. The way you brought Captain Elian and Navigator Chen full circle... the homecoming, the reconciliation, the beautiful symmetry of it all. It's the perfect conclusion to the series."

Pride swells in my chest. "Thank you. That means a lot."

"The emotional depth you've achieved here... it's unlike anything you've written before. There's an authenticity to it that just leaps off the page." She pauses. "Something's changed in your writing. In you."

I glance at a framed picture of Oliver and Lily smiling together on the wall nearby. "Yeah. Something has."

"Well, whatever—or whoever—inspired this transformation, I'm grateful. The sales director is ecstatic. We're already talking about a first printing four times the size of your last book."

"That's fantastic." I can't help but smile. All those weeks of struggling, of staring at blank pages, and now this.

"It gets better," Alison continues, her voice quickening with excitement. "The publicity team has been working overtime, you've probably already seen some of the event invites in your inbox. We've got something big planned, Thomas. Really big."

"Oh?" I take a sip of coffee, watching as Oliver moves to the next plant, sunlight catching in his hair.

"An international book tour. We've expanded the typical eight months to twelve months instead. Twenty-eight countries." She delivers this news with the flourish of someone unveiling a surprise gift.

I nearly choke on my coffee. "Twelve months?"

"I know it sounds intensive, but hear me out. This is the finale to your most successful series. We're talking major media appearances, readings at prestigious venues, literary festivals around the world. London, Paris, Tokyo, Sydney, Berlin, Amsterdam, Munich, Prague—"

"Alison, a year is a long time to be on the road."

"It's the opportunity of a lifetime, Thomas. We're pulling out all the stops. We're talking morning shows, late-night television, podcast appearances. The publicity budget for this is unprecedented."

I sink into a kitchen chair, my mind racing. "When would this start?"

"We'd want to launch right after publication, so about a month from now. The team is already securing venues and accommodations." She pauses. "There's more."

"More?" I echo weakly.

"Paramount has renewed their interest in the film rights, they put down a deposit on the rights last night after we forwarded them the final draft. They want to meet with you in Los Angeles next month. They're talking about a major franchise, Thomas. Multiple films. Streaming spin-offs. They're discussing it with Spielberg. Yeah, that Spielberg! This could be your Harry Potter moment. You'll be able to buy a larger castle than J.K. Rowling once this is all done!"

The kitchen suddenly feels too small, the air too thin. Just a few months ago, this would have been everything I ever wanted—validation, success, the chance to see my creation reach millions more people. But now...

"Thomas? Are you still there?"

"Yeah, sorry. It's just... a lot to take in."

"I know it's overwhelming, but this is what we've been working toward for years. Your career is about to reach a whole new level."

Through the window, I see Oliver look up and smile at me, raising his coffee mug in a little salute. My chest tightens.

"Can I think about it? The tour, I mean."

There's a beat of silence. "Think about it? Thomas, this isn't really optional. The publisher is investing millions in the promotion of this book. They're expecting you to be the face of it."

"I understand that, but twelve months on the road is significant. I've just..." I hesitate, unsure how to explain that I've finally found what I've been writing about all these years. "I've made some changes in my personal life. Important ones."

"Ah." Her tone shifts slightly. "Is this about the bookstore owner? The one Vera mentioned was helping with research?"

I almost laugh at the oversimplification. "It's more than that, Alison. I've moved in with him. And his daughter. We're building a life together."

"That's wonderful, Thomas. Truly. But surely he understands the demands of your career? This tour will set you up financially for the rest of your life. You could buy a bigger house when you return. Travel together during your off-time. Neither of you will ever have to work another day in your lives again!"

"It's not about money."

"Then what is it about?"

"I left him once before. Fifteen years ago. I can't do it again."

"You're not leaving him," Alison says gently. "You're doing your job. Authors go on book tours. It's part of the package."

"Not for a year."

"Look, I understand this is a lot to process. Why don't you discuss it with him? Maybe he and his daughter could join you for parts of the tour. We could work something out."

I rub my forehead. "Maybe."

"Thomas, I need to be clear about something." Her voice takes on a more serious tone. "The general director is expecting this. They've already invested significantly in the planning. Backing out now would have serious implications for your relationship with them. For your career. They could go after you legally if you don't go through with this."

The threat isn't subtle. I've been in this business long enough to understand what she's saying.

"I'll talk to Oliver," I concede. "But I can't promise anything yet."

"That's fair. But I'll need an answer by the end of the week. The publicity team needs to finalize the schedule."

After we hang up, I sit at the kitchen table, staring at my phone. The house is quiet except for the distant sound of the shower running upstairs where Oliver is getting ready for his day at the bookstore.

"Is everything okay?"

I look up to find Lily standing in the doorway, already dressed for school, her backpack slung over one shoulder. I wonder how long she's been there, how much she's heard.

"Just a call from my publisher," I say, forcing a smile. "They really liked the book."

She approaches the table, her expression serious. "I heard you talking about a tour. A really long one."

My stomach sinks. "You heard that, huh?"

She nods, dropping her backpack on the floor and sliding into the chair across from me. "Are you leaving?"

The directness of her question, the slight tremor in her voice, hits me like a physical blow. "I don't know yet. It's complicated."

"But they want you to go away for a year." It's not a question.

"That's what they're proposing, yes."

She looks down at the table, tracing a pattern in the wood grain with her finger. "Dad will pretend it's fine, but it'll break his heart."

I swallow hard. "I know."

"And now you're just going to leave again?" Her eyes meet mine, a mixture of hurt and accusation that makes me flinch.

"I haven't decided anything yet," I tell her. "And whatever I decide, I'll talk it through with both of you first."

"But your publisher is important," she says, an edge to her voice. "And this is a big opportunity. Right?"

The bitterness in her tone is startling from someone usually so supportive. "My career is important," I acknowledge. "But so are you and your dad."

She stands up, grabbing her backpack. "You know what? Just do whatever you want. We were fine before you came back. We'll be fine after you leave."

"Lily, wait—"

But she's already heading for the door. "I'm going to be late for school."

The front door closes with more force than necessary, leaving me alone with the weight of her words. We were fine before you came back. We'll be fine after you leave.

The shower upstairs turns off. In a few minutes, Oliver will come downstairs, and I'll have to tell him about Alison's call, about the tour, about the choice I'm facing. I'll have to look into his eyes and explain that just when we've finally found our way back to each other, the universe seems determined to pull us apart again.

My phone buzzes with a text from Alison: Sending tour itinerary draft. Please review ASAP.

I stare at the message, remembering the excitement in her voice, the promises of success beyond anything I've experienced before. For a moment, I allow myself to imagine it—the packed venues, the interviews, seeing my characters brought to life on screen. Everything I've worked toward for years.

Then I think about Oliver's face when I told him I wasn't leaving again. The trust slowly rebuilding between us. Lily's voice at the dinner table, her stories about school, the way she looks to me now for guidance with her writing.

The sound of Oliver's footsteps on the stairs pulls me from my thoughts. I slip my phone into my pocket and take a deep breath, preparing for a conversation that could change everything—again.

Chapter 17

Oliver

I notice the change in Thomas's demeanour the moment I reach the bottom of the stairs. His shoulders are hunched, his phone clutched tightly in his hand, and his eyes—those expressive eyes that have always revealed everything he tries to hide—are clouded with distress.

"Hey," I say, trying to keep my voice light. "Everything okay?"

Thomas looks up, startled, as if I've caught him in the middle of something illicit. "Oliver, I—" He stops, swallows hard. "That was Alison."

I move to the kitchen counter, pour myself a cup of coffee, needing something to do with my hands. "Your editor? Good news about the manuscript?"

"She loved it." His voice is flat, nothing like the excitement I'd expect. "Said it's the best thing I've ever written."

"That's wonderful," I say, though unease crawls up my spine. Something is wrong. I set my mug down and move closer to him. "Thomas, what is it? What's going on?"

He takes a deep breath. "They want me to do a tour. A big one."

"Well, that's standard, right? For a book release?" I'm missing something here.

"Not like this. Twelve months, Oliver. International. Asia, Europe, Australia, major cities across North America." The words tumble out now. "Plus meetings about potential film adaptations. They're talking about a massive push for this book, calling it the culmination of the series."

Twelve months. The words hang in the air between us.

"I see." My voice sounds distant to my own ears.

"I just heard Lily stomp upstairs. She overheard." Thomas runs a hand through his hair. "She said... she said you two would be fine without me."

The hurt in his voice is palpable, and I want nothing more than to soothe it away. But I need a moment to process this myself. Twelve months. After he just moved in. After we just found each other again.

"When would you leave?" I ask, keeping my voice steady.

"Three weeks. They're expediting everything." Thomas moves toward me, his eyes pleading. "Oliver, I don't know what to do. I promised I wouldn't leave again."

I take his hands in mine, forcing myself to look directly into his eyes. "This isn't the same as before, Thomas. This is your career, your work. The work you've poured yourself into for fifteen years."

"But what about us? What about what we've built?" His voice cracks. "I just found you again."

"And you'll find me when you come back." The words feel like stones in my mouth, heavy and hard to push out, but I force them anyway. "We're not kids anymore. This isn't you leaving for college with no plan to return. This is your life's work being celebrated."

Thomas shakes his head. "I can negotiate. Maybe I can get them down to six months instead of twelve. Or breaks between legs of the tour where I can come home." He doesn't sound confident.

Home. The word warms me even as the situation chills me to the bone.

"You should go," I say firmly, though everything inside me screams against it. "The full tour. Do everything they're asking."

"Oliver—"

"No, listen to me." I squeeze his hands. "I've read your books. All of them. I know what Captain Elian means to you, what Navigator Chen represents. This is the culmination of our story too, in a way. You need to be there to see it through."

"But what about Lily? She's already upset."

I sigh, thinking of my daughter's reaction. "I'll talk to her. She's thirteen and dramatic, but she's also smart and compassionate. She'll understand."

"Will she?" Thomas looks doubtful. "Will you? Really understand?"

I release his hands and turn away, needing a moment where he can't read my expression. The truth is, I don't want him to go, I'm lying through my teeth. Not for twelve days, let alone twelve months. Not when we've just found our rhythm, when Thomas has become such an integral part of our lives that the thought of our home without him feels wrong.

But I also know what his writing means to him. What this book means.

"Do you remember," I say, turning back to face him, "when we were seventeen, and you told me about Captain Elian for the first time? We were at the cove, lying on that old blanket you always kept in your car."

Thomas nods, a small smile playing at the corners of his mouth despite the tension. "You said it sounded like Star Trek meets The Odyssey."

"And you got so excited explaining how it was different." I can't help but smile at the memory. "Your whole face lit up. I'd never seen anyone so passionate about anything before."

"I was a nerdy kid with big dreams."

"You were beautiful," I correct him. "And you still are when you talk about your work. This tour—it's the climax of everything you've worked for. Everything you dreamed about back then."

"But my dreams have changed," Thomas says quietly. "They include you now. And Lily."

"We're not going anywhere." I step closer to him. "Think of it this way—you spent fifteen years writing about us finding our way back to each other. Now we have. That part of the story is written. But there are other chapters that need to be lived too."

"I hate the thought of being away from you for so long."

"I hate it too," I admit, finally allowing some of my true feelings to surface. "But I'd hate myself more if I asked you to stay and you resented me for it later."

"I could never resent you, Oliver."

"You say that now. But what happens six months from now when your book is climbing the charts and you're missing key promotional opportunities? When the film people want meetings and you're trapped here ordering inventory for the store?"

Thomas is silent, and I know my words have hit home.

"I want you to go," I say, the lie burning my throat. "I want you to have this moment. You've earned it."

"What about us?"

"We'll be here." I step closer, wrap my arms around his waist. "There's video calls and texting. Holidays and breaks in the schedule. We'll make it work."

"You sound so certain." Thomas's arms encircle me, his chin resting on my shoulder.

I'm not certain. I'm terrified. But I won't tell him that.

"I am certain," I say instead. "About us. About you. About what we can handle."

Thomas pulls back slightly to look at me. "What about Lily?"

"I'll talk to her. She adores you, Thomas. She wants what's best for you too."

"I should be the one to talk to her," he says. "To explain."

"We'll do it together." I press my forehead against his. "That's what families do."

The word 'families' hangs between us, heavy with meaning. Is that what we are now? A family? The thought both comforts and terrifies me.

"I'm still not convinced," Thomas says. "Twelve months is a long time."

"It is," I agree. "But we waited fifteen years to find each other again. What's one more?"

Thomas's laugh is strained. "When did you become the optimist in this relationship?"

"One of us has to be." I kiss him softly. "And you've been carrying that torch long enough."

We stand there in the kitchen, holding each other, the reality of our impending separation settling around us like dust. I want to tell him not to go. I want to beg him to stay. But I can't. I won't. Because I love him too much to clip his wings just when he's finally ready to soar.

"I should call Alison back," Thomas says eventually. "Tell her I'm in."

"Yes, you should." I step back, creating space between us that feels like practice for the months to come.

Thomas picks up his phone from the counter, stares at it for a long moment. "Are you sure about this, Oliver? Really sure?"

No, I'm not sure. I'm not sure at all.

"I'm sure," I say firmly. "Make the call."

Thomas nods, dials the number, puts the phone to his ear. I turn away, busying myself with rinsing out coffee mugs in the sink, giving him privacy for the conversation while staying close enough to offer silent support.

"Alison? It's Thomas." His voice sounds stronger now, more

resolved. "About the tour... I'm in. All of it. The whole twelve months."

I grip the edge of the sink, knuckles white, as he continues the conversation, discussing details and logistics. Each word is another step toward his departure, another day added to our separation. But I keep my back straight, my breathing even. This is what's best for him. For his career. For the story he's been telling for fifteen years.

When he hangs up, I've composed myself enough to turn and offer him a smile. "All set?"

"All set." He looks shell-shocked. "I leave November 1st. New York first, then Chicago, LA, Seattle, Vancouver..."

"Sounds exciting," I say, the words hollow in my mouth.

"It won't be. Not without you and Lily."

I cross the kitchen to him, take his face in my hands. "Then we'll make sure the next three weeks are so good you'll have plenty to remember while you're gone."

Thomas leans into my touch. "I'm going to miss you so much."

"I know." I brush my thumb across his cheek. "I'll miss you too. But this is right, Thomas. This is what needs to happen."

"How can you be so sure?"

Because I've spent fifteen years learning how to let you go, I think but don't say. Instead, I kiss him, pouring everything I can't articulate into the contact.

"I'm sure," I whisper against his lips, "because some things are worth waiting for. And you, Thomas Winters, have always been worth the wait."

He wraps his arms around me, holding me so tightly it almost hurts. I cling to him just as desperately, memorizing the feel of him, the scent of him, the warmth of his body against mine. For a moment, I allow myself to acknowledge the dread pooling in my stomach, the fear that once he leaves, everything will change again.

But then I push it away. This isn't like before. We're not teenagers making impossible promises. We're adults who have found our way back to each other against all odds. We can survive twelve months apart.

We have to.

Chapter 18

Thomas

Two weeks pass like water through my fingers. Each morning, I wake beside Oliver, memorizing the lines of his face, the rhythm of his breathing. Each night, I help Lily with her writing, watching her story grow stronger, more confident. And every hour in between, I'm packing, planning, preparing to leave them both.

"Your train tickets arrived," Oliver says, sliding an envelope across the kitchen counter. His voice is steady, practical. Too practical. "I printed your itinerary too."

"Thanks." I take the envelope without opening it. "You didn't have to do that."

He shrugs, turning back to the coffee maker. "Wanted to make sure everything's in order."

I've noticed this new distance in him—slight but unmistakable. The way he talks about my departure with such calm efficiency. The way he's stopped mentioning Christmas plans or anything beyond November 1st. As if he's already practising for my absence.

"We should celebrate tonight," I suggest. "Maybe that Italian place Lily likes?"

"I have inventory to finish at the store." He pours coffee into my mug, not meeting my eyes. "Maybe this weekend."

But this weekend will bring more preparations, more distance. We're running out of time, and Oliver is already building walls to protect himself. I recognize the technique—I've spent fifteen years writing about characters who do exactly this.

"I'll help with inventory," I offer. "We can order in."

He nods, but I can see he's already somewhere else, somewhere I can't reach.

* * *

"Is this where you want these?" I hold up a stack of new releases, standing in the fiction section of Harbour Books.

Oliver glances up from his clipboard. "Second display table, front facing."

We work in silence, moving through the store with practiced efficiency. In just two months, I've learned the rhythms of this place—when to restock the bestsellers, how Oliver likes the staff picks arranged, which customers prefer recommendations and which want to browse undisturbed.

"Did Lily say when she'd be home?" I ask, breaking the quiet.

"Study group until seven."

"She's been spending a lot of time there lately."

Oliver pauses, his hand resting on a stack of books. "She's withdrawing. It's what she does when she's worried about losing someone."

The words hit me like a physical blow. "Oliver—"

"It's fine, Thomas. We understand. This tour is important."

"You and Lily are important."

He nods, but doesn't look convinced. "We'll be here when you get back."

The promise hangs between us, fragile as spider silk. I want to believe him, but I see the doubt in his eyes. The same doubt that lives in mine.

Later, I find Lily's notebook abandoned on the kitchen table. Her story about Mira sits open, the pages covered in her neat handwriting. I shouldn't read it without permission, but a sentence catches my eye:

Mira stood at the edge of the star field, torn between the light of distant worlds and the warmth of the one she called home.

My throat tightens. Even at thirteen, Lily understands the choice I'm facing better than I do.

* * *

The suitcase lies open on our bed, half-filled with clothes for every season. Twelve months of my life condensed into luggage that will follow me across oceans.

"Did you pack the power adapters?" Oliver asks from the doorway.

"First thing in." I hold up a travel case. "And extra medication. And those protein bars you insisted on."

He smiles, but it doesn't reach his eyes. "Always prepared."

"I learned from the best. Navigator Chen was famously over-prepared."

The mention of my character—his character—usually brings a flush to his cheeks, but today he just nods.

I watch him place the shirt in my suitcase, his movements deliberate, controlled. This is how Oliver processes pain—through practical action, through preparation. He's preparing himself for my absence by creating a life that doesn't depend on my presence.

"I'll call every day, we'll video chat every night" I promise.

"We'll be fine, Thomas." He zips a compartment closed with finality. "It's just a year."

Just a year. Twelve months. Three hundred and sixty-five days of waking up without him. Of missing Lily's writing breakthroughs, her school events, her growing up.

Just a year of living the life I've written about for fifteen years—a traveller searching for something I've already found.

* * *

Three days before my departure, I find myself alone in the writing nook at Harbour Books. Oliver is running errands, Lily is at school, and the store doesn't open for another hour.

I open my laptop, intending to answer emails from my publicist, but instead find myself opening Lily's contest submission. She'd asked me to review it one last time before the deadline.

Mira's Choice is the title. A story about a girl who discovers that stars contain memories, including those of her mother who died years before. The story follows Mira as she's offered a chance to journey among the stars, collecting these memories—but at the cost of leaving her father alone.

I read through the pages, struck by the maturity of Lily's prose, the depth of her understanding. Near the end, a passage stops me cold:

"The stars will always be there," Mira told the Keeper. "But my father is here now. And he needs me as much as I need him."

The Keeper nodded slowly. "The universe offers many paths, but only you can choose which one leads home."

Mira looked up at the glittering sky, then back at the small house where her father waited. And she knew, with sudden clarity, that some journeys matter more than others.

I sit back, the words echoing in my mind. Some journeys matter more than others.

For fifteen years, I've written about Captain Elian searching for a home she left behind. For fifteen years, I've been doing the same— living in the regret of what I abandoned when I left Harbour Point. Left

Oliver.

And now, history is repeating itself. I'm choosing to leave again, for success, for career, for the dream I've chased since I was seventeen.

But what if I'm chasing the wrong dream?

I pull out my phone and dial a number I've been avoiding.

"Vera speaking."

"It's Thomas." My voice is steadier than I expected. "We need to talk about the tour."

"Thomas! I was just about to call you. The London team wants to add three more stops, and—"

"I'm not going, Vera."

A beat of silence. "Excuse me?"

"I'm not doing the tour. Not for twelve months."

"Thomas, this isn't negotiable. The publisher has invested—"

"I'll do a shortened tour. Two months, three at most. But I'm not leaving for a year."

Her laugh is sharp, disbelieving. "You can't be serious. This is the opportunity of a lifetime. Your career—"

"I've spent fifteen years writing about a character who never found her way home," I cut in. "I'm not making that mistake again."

"This is about the bookstore owner again, isn't it? And his daughter?" Her voice hardens. "Thomas, you need to be reasonable. They'll be there when you get back."

"That's what I told myself fifteen years ago." I stand up, pacing the small nook. "I left once, convinced myself it was temporary. It cost me fifteen years. I won't do it again."

"The publisher won't accept this. There will be consequences, Thomas. Serious ones."

"Then I'll face them."

"We could lose the film deal. The international rights. Everything we've worked for all these years."

I think of Oliver in our kitchen, carefully avoiding talk of the future. Of Lily, withdrawing to protect herself from another loss.

"Some things matter more," I say simply.

"I'll give you twenty-four hours to reconsider," she says, her voice clipped. "Think about what you're throwing away."

"I'm not throwing anything away. I'm choosing what to keep."

I end the call and sit in the quiet of the bookstore, surrounded by stories of adventure and escape. For years, I've been one of those stories—the writer who left his hometown, found success in distant cities, lived the dream.

But the real story, I realize, has always been here. In the spaces between leaving and returning. In the quiet moments with Oliver and Lily that mean more than any book tour ever could.

Chapter 19

Thomas

I sit in the quiet bookstore, my decision settling around me like a familiar weight. Not the burden I'd feared, but something steadying. Right.

The bell above the door chimes, and Oliver walks in carrying a cardboard tray with coffee cups. His face brightens when he sees me.

"You're here early," he says, setting the tray on the counter. "I brought you that hazelnut thing you like."

He looks relaxed today in a simple blue sweater that makes his eyes seem deeper. He hasn't started bracing himself for my departure yet—that would come later, closer to November 1st. The date looms in my mind like a deadline for disaster.

"Thanks," I say, taking the coffee. "I was reading Lily's final draft."

"And? Is it ready for submission?"

"More than ready."

I take a deep breath. "Can we talk for a minute? Before you open?"

Something in my tone makes his expression shift. "Everything okay?"

"Yeah. Better than okay, actually."

He follows me to the reading nook in the back, where comfortable chairs form a small circle around a low table. The space feels intimate, protected from the rest of the world by tall bookshelves. I've come to think of it as our sanctuary.

Oliver sits across from me, his posture tense. "What's going on?"

I meet his eyes directly. "I called Vera this morning. I'm not going on the tour."

His coffee cup freezes halfway to his mouth. "What?"

"I'm not leaving for twelve months. I told her I'd do a shortened version—two months, maybe three. But that's it."

Oliver sets his cup down carefully, like it might shatter. "Thomas... you can't do that."

"I already did."

"But the publisher—your contract—"

"I don't care about the contract."

"You should care." His voice rises slightly. "This is your career we're talking about. Your life's work."

"No." I lean forward, needing him to understand. "My life's work is sitting right in front of me. It's you and Lily and what we're building together."

Oliver shakes his head, confusion etched across his face. "You don't have to choose. We'll be fine for a year. We can visit, call every day—"

"That's what I told myself fifteen years ago," I interrupt, the words spilling out faster now. "That it wasn't really leaving because I'd come back. That we could make it work with phone calls and visits. And it cost us fifteen years, Oliver. Fifteen years I can never get back."

"This is different."

"Is it? Because it feels exactly the same." I run a hand through my hair, frustrated that he doesn't see it. "I'm on the verge of making the same dumb mistake twice, and I can't do it. I won't."

Oliver's expression softens. "Thomas, you're not that scared kid anymore. You're not running away from anything."

"Aren't I? Because it feels like I'm running toward success and away from what really matters. Again."

"But your book—the movie rights—"

"I don't care." The certainty in my voice surprises even me. "None of that matters if I lose you again."

Oliver stares at me, his eyes searching mine. "What did Vera say?"

"That there will be consequences. Serious ones." I shrug. "Let there be."

"They could drop you entirely. Sue for breach of contract."

"Then they can have the advance back. I've got savings."

"The movie deal could fall through."

"Then it falls through."

Oliver's hands tighten around his coffee cup. "You're being reckless."

"No, I'm finally being clear about what matters." I reach across and take his hands in mine. "Oliver, I've spent fifteen years writing about a character who lost her way home. Who sacrificed love for duty and has been searching for a way back ever since. I wrote that story because it was mine."

His fingers tremble slightly in my grasp.

"But here's the thing," I continue. "Captain Elian finally finds her way back. She finally chooses love over duty. And if my character can be that brave, then so can I."

Oliver's eyes shine with unshed tears. "You can't throw away everything you've worked for. I won't let you."

"I'm not throwing anything away. I'm choosing what to keep." I squeeze his hands. "Reading Lily's story this morning—she understands something I've only just figured out. That some journeys matter more than others."

"Thomas—"

"I love you, Oliver Chen. I've loved you since we were teenagers, hiding among these books. I never stopped. Not when I left, not when I tried to forget, not when I poured it all into my writing instead." My voice cracks. "And I'm not leaving again."

Oliver pulls one hand free to wipe at his eyes. "You stubborn, impossible man."

"That's me."

"What about the legal issues? The publisher could—"

"Let them try. I'll write another book. Ten more books. But I'll write them here, with you and Lily."

"The money—"

"I don't care about the money." I laugh, the freedom of it bubbling up from somewhere deep. "Don't you get it? None of that matters if I can't be with the man I love."

Oliver stands abruptly, turning away from me. For a terrible moment, I think I've pushed too far, said too much. Then I realize he's walking to the front door. He flips the sign to "Closed" and locks it with a decisive click.

When he turns back to me, his expression has changed entirely. Gone is the practical bookstore owner worried about contracts and consequences. In his place stands the boy I fell in love with—eyes dark with desire, a predatory smile playing at the corners of his mouth.

"You're really staying?" he asks, his voice dropping to a register that sends heat straight to my groin.

I stand to meet him, already half-hard with anticipation. "I'm really staying."

"Because of us?"

"Because of us."

He crosses the distance between us in three quick strides. His hands find my face, thumbs roughly tracing my cheekbones before sliding into my hair, gripping tightly enough to make me gasp.

"I never thought I'd hear you say that," he whispers, his breath hot against my lips. "I never let myself hope."

"Hope now," I tell him, my hands finding his hips, pulling him against me so he can feel my growing arousal. "Hope for everything."

His mouth crashes into mine with an urgency that speaks of years of longing. His tongue demands entrance, which I eagerly grant, moaning as he explores me thoroughly. I pull him closer, my hands sliding beneath his sweater to find the warm skin beneath, raking my nails down his back. We stumble backward until my legs hit the reading chair, and I sink into it, pulling Oliver down to straddle my lap.

"We're in the store," he murmurs against my neck, even as he grinds down against my hardness.

"It's closed," I remind him, already working at the button of his jeans, dragging the zipper down with deliberate slowness.

"Anyone could look through the window—"

"Not back here. Not behind all these shelves." I slip my hand inside his jeans, finding him hot and hard, already leaking through his boxers. "Just like that time after hours when we were seventeen. Remember? Right against these very bookshelves."

His laugh vibrates against my throat where he's sucking what will definitely be a visible mark tomorrow. "God, yes. My dad nearly caught us. You had to hide behind the fantasy section with your pants around your ankles."

"Worth it," I say, squeezing him through the thin cotton, delighting in his sharp intake of breath. "Though I think I've improved my technique since then."

Oliver pulls back just enough to look at me, his pupils blown wide with lust. "You're really not leaving?"

"I'm really not leaving." I tug his jeans and boxers down his hips in one swift motion. "Now, I need you to fuck me on this chair before I lose my mind."

Something shifts in his expression then—a final wall coming down, replaced by raw hunger. He kisses me again, bruising in its intensity, his hands making quick work of my belt and zipper. I lift my hips to help him strip me, gasping when cool air hits my exposed cock.

"Turn around," Oliver commands, his voice rough with need. "Hands on the armrests."

I comply eagerly, positioning myself on my knees on the chair, facing the backrest with my ass presented to him. I hear the distinctive sound of a cap opening and glance over my shoulder to see Oliver slicking his fingers with lube.

"You carry that in your pocket?" I ask, amused despite my desperation.

"Since we started sleeping together," he admits, circling my entrance with a slick finger. "I've learned to be prepared around you, Thomas."

The first breach of his finger makes me drop my head between my shoulders, a low moan escaping me. Oliver works me open with practiced efficiency, adding a second finger, then a third, finding that spot inside me that makes my cock jerk and leak.

"Please," I beg, pushing back against his hand. "I need you inside me. Now."

Oliver withdraws his fingers, leaving me empty and aching. I feel the blunt head of his cock pressing against my prepared entrance, hot and insistent.

"Look at me," he demands, gripping my hair to turn my face toward him. "I want to see your eyes when I take you."

Our gazes lock as he pushes forward, the exquisite stretch of him entering me drawing a strangled cry from my throat. Oliver's face is a study in pleasure and restraint as he sinks into me inch by delicious inch. When he's fully seated within me, we both pause, adjusting to the overwhelming sensation.

"You feel incredible," he breathes against my ear, his chest pressed to my back. "So tight around me. Like you were made for this—for me."

His words send shivers down my spine. "Move," I plead. "Please, Oliver. I need you to move."

He establishes a punishing rhythm, each thrust driving deeper than the last. The old reading chair creaks beneath us, the sound mixing with our harsh breathing and the obscene slap of skin against skin. My neglected cock bobs between my legs, dripping pre-cum onto the upholstery.

"Touch yourself," Oliver commands, his pace faltering slightly as he fights his approaching climax. "I want to feel you come around me."

I reach between my legs, wrapping my hand around my aching length, stroking in time with his thrusts. The dual sensation is overwhelming— Oliver hitting that perfect spot inside me while my hand works my shaft.

"This is what I've wanted since you walked back into my store," he confesses, his rhythm becoming erratic. "You, choosing us over everything else."

"Nothing compares to this," I gasp, feeling my orgasm building at the base of my spine. "To us. To what we have."

My release hits me with stunning intensity, my body clenching around Oliver as I paint the chair beneath us with hot stripes of cum. The feeling of me tightening around him pushes Oliver over the edge, and he drives into me one final time, emptying himself deep inside me with a guttural groan, his forehead pressed between my shoulder blades.

We stay joined for long moments, our breathing slowly returning to normal. Eventually, Oliver withdraws carefully and helps me turn around, pulling me into his lap, his arms wrapping around me possessively.

"Thomas," he murmurs, my name a reverent whisper on his lips.

"I'm here," I promise, pressing my forehead to his. "I'm staying right here."

Afterwards, we hold each other in the oversized chair, our bodies still humming with residual pleasure. Oliver's head rests against my chest, his hair tickling my chin. Outside, the world continues—people walk past the store windows, cars drive by—but in here, time seems suspended.

"We should probably clean up before we open the store," Oliver says eventually, though he makes no move to disentangle himself from me. "It's almost nine."

I laugh softly, pressing a kiss to the top of his head. "Probably. Though I'm tempted to keep you right here all morning."

Oliver looks up at me, his eyes soft with something that goes beyond desire. "We have time now," he says, his thumb tracing my lower lip. "All the time we need."

The promise in those words fills me with a joy more profound than even our physical connection. After years apart, we finally have the luxury of time—to rediscover each other, to build something lasting, to write our story together.

"All the time we need," I echo, sealing the promise with a kiss. "Let them wait."

He laughs softly. "Easy for you to say. You don't have bills to pay."

"We'll pay them together." I press a kiss to the top of his head. "Everything together from now on."

Oliver sits up, looking at me with renewed seriousness. "Are you absolutely certain about the tour? We could find a compromise—maybe six months instead of twelve?"

I shake my head. "Three months, maximum. That's my final offer."

"Your publisher will fight you on this."

"Let them. I've got a pretty good story about finding my way home. People might want to read it."

Oliver smiles, tracing my jawline with his fingertip. "You're really choosing us over your career."

"I'm choosing to have both—just not at the expense of what matters most."

He kisses me again, softly this time. "When did you get so wise?"

"I learned it from a navigator who waited fifteen years for his captain to figure out what really mattered." I catch his hand, pressing it against my heart. "I'm not making him wait any longer."

* * *

Lily

I can tell something's up the moment I walk through the door. Dad and Thomas are sitting at the kitchen table, hands clasped together on top, wearing these weird matching smiles that scream "we have news." My stomach drops. I've been trying not to think about Thomas leaving—the tour, the twelve months away, the inevitable goodbye that's been hanging over our house like a storm cloud.

"Hey, stargazer," Thomas says, using the nickname he gave me after our night watching the Perseids.

"How was school?" Dad asks, but his voice has that forced casualness that parents use when they're stalling.

I drop my backpack by the door. "Fine. What's going on?"

They exchange a look—that private language they've developed over the past few months. Dad nods at Thomas, giving him permission for something.

"I called Vera this morning," Thomas says, leaning forward. "I'm not going on the tour."

The words don't compute at first. "What?"

"I'm staying here. In Harbour Point. With you and your dad."

"But... your book. The movie deal. Everything you've worked for." My voice comes out smaller than I intended.

Thomas shakes his head. "None of that matters if I'm not with the people I love."

Dad's eyes are suspiciously bright. "Thomas and I talked it through. He's going to do some virtual events, maybe a few weekend trips to major cities, but nothing that takes him away for more than a few days at a time."

"Won't you get in trouble?" I ask Thomas. "With your publisher?"

"Vera wasn't happy," Thomas admits. "But we'll figure it out. Some things are worth fighting for."

The relief hits me so hard I have to sit down. Thomas isn't leaving. He's staying here, with us. Our family stays whole.

"I thought..." My voice catches. "I thought you were going to tell me you were leaving sooner."

Dad reaches for my hand. "We would never spring that on you, Lily."

"I know what it's like to be left behind," Thomas says quietly. "I wouldn't do that to either of you."

Something about his words makes me realize the magnitude of what he's giving up. For us. For me. The weight of it settles on my shoulders—not crushing, but significant. What if someday he regrets this choice?

"Are you sure?" I ask. "What if your book doesn't do as well because you stayed?"

Thomas laughs. "Then I'll write another one. Right here at that desk we set up at Harbour Books."

"Speaking of which," Dad says, standing up, "I should probably go check on the store. Maria's been alone all afternoon."

After Dad leaves, Thomas and I sit in comfortable silence for a minute. I'm still processing everything.

"Want to work on your competition entry?" Thomas asks finally. "Deadline's coming up soon, right?"

I nod. "Friday."

"Let's take a look, then."

We move to the living room, where I've spread out my drafts across the coffee table. Thomas sits cross-legged on the floor, sorting through the pages with careful hands.

"You've made incredible progress," he says, reading through my latest revision. "Mira's journey feels so real now."

"I changed the ending," I tell him, pointing to the final pages. "She doesn't just find her mom's memories in the stars. She realizes she's been carrying them inside her all along."

Thomas reads the new conclusion, his expression softening. "This is beautiful, Lily. Really beautiful."

"I was thinking about Mom when I wrote it." I pull my knees up to my chest. "And about you."

"Me?"

"Yeah. About how sometimes the things we're searching for are already with us. We just don't recognize them."

Thomas sets the pages down carefully. "That's a profound insight for someone your age."

"I'm not a little kid," I remind him.

"No, you're definitely not." He smiles. "You're a writer."

The way he says it—like it's already true, not something I'm trying to become—makes my chest warm with pride.

"Can I ask you something?" I say, picking at a loose thread on my jeans.

"Anything."

"Do you really not mind giving up the tour? Being famous and travelling everywhere?"

Thomas leans back against the couch, considering. "When I was your age, all I wanted was to escape this town. I thought success meant being somewhere else, being someone else."

"But now?"

"Now I know that success is finding where you belong." He gestures around the room. "Who you belong with."

"Dad and me?"

"Dad and you." He nods. "I spent fifteen years writing about characters searching across galaxies for home. Turns out, mine was right where I left it."

I think about my story, about Mira and her journey through the stars. "In my story, Mira realizes that home isn't just a place. It's the people who know your story."

"That's exactly right." Thomas picks up my manuscript again. "And speaking of stories, let's make sure this one is perfect for the competition."

We spend the next hour fine-tuning sentences and strengthening descriptions. Thomas doesn't rewrite anything—he just asks questions that help me see what needs fixing.

"How does Mira feel when she first realizes the stars are talking to her?"

"What does the constellation look like when it takes the shape of her mother?"

"What's the sound of starlight in her mind?"

His questions push me to dig deeper, to find the specific details that make the story come alive. By the time we finish, "The Memory of Stars" feels more real to me than ever.

"You know," Thomas says as we organize the final pages, "I have a strong suspicion that you're going to do better than I did in this competition."

"What if I don't win either?"

"Then you'll keep writing anyway, because that's what writers do." He taps the manuscript. "But this story has something special, Lily. It has heart."

"Do you think Mom would have liked it?"

Thomas's expression softens. "Your dad tells me she loved the stars almost as much as you do. I think she would have been incredibly proud."

"Sometimes I worry I'll forget her," I admit, the words tumbling out before I can stop them. "That's why Mira is so desperate to find her mom's memories. I'm afraid someday I won't remember what Mom's laugh sounded like."

Thomas doesn't offer empty reassurances. Instead, he says, "That's why we write, Lily. To preserve the things we're afraid of losing."

I think about all the notebooks I've filled with memories of Mom—her cookie recipes, the way she braided my hair, the bedtime stories she made up. "I guess I've been doing that."

"And now you're turning those memories into something new. Something that might help other kids who've lost someone."

The idea that my story could matter to someone else—could help them feel less alone—makes me sit up straighter.

"I think it's ready," I decide, gathering the pages together. "For the competition."

"I think so too."

We hear the front door open, and Dad calls out, "I brought dinner! Maria insisted we needed celebration food."

Thomas winks at me. "Shall we tell him the story's finished?"

"Not yet." I carefully place my manuscript in a folder. "I want to surprise him when I submit it."

* * *

The next morning, I wake up early. The house is quiet—Dad and Thomas are still asleep. I tiptoe downstairs with my folder and sit at the computer in the living room.

The Young Writers of America website is already open in my browser.

I click on "Submit Entry" and follow the instructions, carefully typing my information and uploading my story.

Title: The Memory of Stars

Author: Lily Chen

Age Category: 13-15

My finger hovers over the submit button. Once I press it, my words will be out there in the world, being read by strangers. The thought makes my stomach flip.

I think about what Thomas said—about writing to preserve what we're afraid of losing. About stories having the power to help others feel less alone.

I think about Mom, and how she always told me to be brave.

I click submit.

The confirmation page appears: "Thank you, Lily Chen. Your entry has been received."

A strange calm washes over me. Whether I win or not doesn't matter as much as it did before. I wrote the story I needed to write. I found the words to keep Mom's memory alive, not just for me, but maybe for someone else who needs them.

I hear movement upstairs—Dad or Thomas getting up. Soon they'll come downstairs and we'll have breakfast together, like we do every morning now. Thomas will talk about his writing plans for the day. Dad will go over the bookstore schedule. I'll tell them I submitted my story, and they'll both be proud.

This is what Thomas gave up his tour for. Not fame or fortune, but ordinary mornings like this one. Pancakes and coffee and family conversation.

I close the laptop and head to the kitchen to start the coffee, feeling a new confidence settle inside me. I am Lily Chen. Daughter. Writer. Keeper of memories.

Chapter 20

Thomas

I stare at my phone, half-expecting it to burst into flames. It's been two weeks since I told Vera I wasn't going on the international tour. Two weeks of silence that speaks volumes about her disappointment. The screen lights up with her name, and I take a deep breath before answering.

"Thomas Winters."

"You stubborn, impossible man." Vera's voice holds none of its usual warmth. "Do you have any idea what I've been dealing with?"

"I can imagine." I lean against the counter in Harbour Books, watching Oliver help a customer across the room. He glances over, concern etching his features.

"No, you can't. The publisher is furious. The marketing team is in shambles. And I've spent fourteen days trying to salvage your career."

I close my eyes. "I appreciate that, Vera. I do."

"Do you?" Her sigh crackles through the phone. "Look, I understand why you're doing this. I do. But this is business, Thomas. Your contract—"

"I know about the contract."

"Then you know they could sue you for breach."

The weight of that possibility sits heavy on my chest. I've been trying not to think about it, focusing instead on the quiet mornings with Oliver, helping Lily with her homework, the rhythm we've created together. "Are they going to?"

Another sigh. "That's why I'm calling. I've been in meetings all week. I think I've found a compromise."

I straighten. "I'm listening."

"Weekend events. Major cities only, primarily domestic with a few key international appearances. Virtual sessions for the smaller markets. You'd be gone no more than two or three days at a time."

"How long overall?"

"Six months instead of twelve. You'd be home most weeks. The times you're away the publisher will pay for the bookseller and his kid to come with you. They'll even compensate for lost income at his store."

I watch as Oliver rings up the customer's purchase, his smile genuine as he hands over a bag of books. This is what I chose—this life, this man, this family we're building. But I also chose to be a writer long ago.

"The publisher is willing to accept this?" I ask.

"Not willingly. But they're also not eager for the PR nightmare of suing their star author for wanting to be with his family and the inspiration for his stories. Plus, your manuscript is exceptional, Thomas. They want it to succeed."

"And the film deal?"

"Still on the table. Spielberg said he'll work around your schedule for meetings."

I exhale slowly. "Weekends only. Home during the week."

"Yes. And we'll cluster the international appearances so you're not crossing oceans for a single event."

Oliver approaches, eyebrows raised in question. I cover the phone. "It's Vera. She has a compromise."

He nods, squeezing my shoulder before giving me privacy.

"Thomas? Are you still there?" Vera asks.

"I'm here. This sounds... workable."

"It's more than workable. It's an absolute fucking miracle I pulled off for you, you ungrateful little shit." Her tone softens. "You've found something special there, haven't you?"

I watch Oliver arranging a display of new releases, his movements precise and thoughtful. "Yes. Something I should have never left behind in the first place."

"Well, don't mess it up this time. I need your answer by tomorrow so I can finalize the revised schedule."

"You'll have it. And Vera? Thank you."

After hanging up, I find Oliver in the storeroom, unpacking a shipment of books.

"So?" he asks, setting aside a hardcover.

"Weekends only. Home during the week. Six months instead of twelve."

Relief washes over his face. "That's... that's good, right?"

"It's better than good. It means I can fulfill my obligations without leaving you and Lily. They'll even pay to fly you and Lily with me."

Oliver steps closer, his hands finding mine. "I told you we'd figure it out."

"You did. I just wasn't sure the publisher would agree."

"Your agent must be formidable."

I laugh. "Vera? She's terrifying. But she's also the best advocate I could ask for."

Oliver's fingers trace patterns on my palms. "So what does this mean for your daily schedule? For us?"

The question makes me pause. I've been so focused on not leaving that I haven't thought about what staying actually looks like—how to balance my career with this new life.

"I'll still write, of course. But I'm thinking about something else too."

The idea has been forming since I decided to stay, a way to bridge my two worlds.

"What's that?"

"A writing workshop. Here at Harbour Books."

Oliver's eyes widen. "A workshop?"

"Once a week. For aspiring writers in the community." I gesture around us. "We already have the space. And it would bring in customers."

"You'd teach it?"

"Who better? And it would give me purpose here beyond just being 'the author who's boinking the bookstore owner.'"

Oliver laughs. "Is that how you see yourself?"

"Sometimes. I want to contribute, Oliver. To your life, to Harbour Books. This could be my way."

He considers this, eyes thoughtful. "We could use the reading nook on Wednesday evenings. It's our slowest night."

"So that's a yes?"

Instead of answering, he pulls me close, his lips finding mine in a kiss that feels like home and adventure all at once.

"Yes," he whispers against my mouth. "It's always yes with you."

* * *

"Welcome to the first Harbour Books Writing Workshop." I look around at the circle of faces—twelve participants ranging from teenagers to retirees, all clutching notebooks and pens with varying degrees of nervousness and eagerness. "I'm Thomas Winters, and I'll be your guide on this journey."

It's been three weeks since Vera called with the compromise. I've already completed my first weekend of appearances—a whirlwind trip to Chicago and Detroit that left me exhausted but satisfied. Coming home to Oliver and Lily made the travel worthwhile.

Now, standing in the reading nook of Harbour Books on a Wednesday evening, I feel a different kind of satisfaction blooming.

"Before we begin, I want to set some ground rules." I perch on the edge of a table. "First, this is a safe space. Your words matter here. Second, writing is rewriting—nothing is perfect the first time. And third, the only way to become a writer is to write."

A young woman with purple hair raises her hand. "Even if it's terrible?"

"Especially if it's terrible," I grin. "My first draft of The Navigator's Star was so bad my editor threatened to quit on the spot."

Laughter ripples through the group, easing the tension.

"Now, let's start with introductions. Tell us your name and what brings you here tonight."

One by one, they share their stories. A high school teacher who dreams of writing historical fiction. A retired fisherman documenting the changing coastline. A nurse crafting mystery novels during night shifts.

And Lily, sitting proudly in the front row, her notebook already filled with ideas.

"I'm Lily Chen," she announces when her turn comes. "I'm working on a science fiction story about stars that hold memories. And I'm here because writing makes me feel connected to my mom, and because Thomas is basically family now."

Her words catch me off guard, warmth spreading through my chest. From the back of the room, where Oliver is pretending to organize books while eavesdropping, I see him pause, his eyes meeting mine with equal surprise and joy.

"Thank you, Lily," I manage, my voice slightly rough. "That's... that's a beautiful reason to write."

As the workshop progresses, I guide them through exercises on character development and sensory details. Their pens scratch against paper, faces intent with concentration. This is different from writing alone in my cottage—it's creation shared, multiplied by each person in the circle.

"Remember," I tell them as our time draws to a close, "writing isn't just about publishing or fame. It's about finding your voice, telling your story. Sometimes the most important reader is yourself."

After everyone files out with promises to return next week, Oliver approaches, sliding his arms around my waist.

"Professor Winters," he teases. "Very impressive."

"Was it okay? I was nervous they'd expect some grand wisdom about publishing."

"You gave them something better. Permission to write for the joy of it." He nods toward Lily, who's chatting animatedly with the purple-haired woman. "And you've made quite an impression on our daughter."

Oliver's declaration catches me off guard, the word "our" reverberating through me like a struck bell. "Family," I echo Lily's earlier words, the syllables feeling both foreign and familiar on my tongue. "She called me family."

Oliver's eyes soften, a vulnerability there I've come to treasure. "Is that okay?"

"It's more than okay. It's everything."

He kisses me quickly, mindful of the few lingering customers. "So, how does it feel? Finding this balance?"

I consider the question, thinking about the weekend appearances ahead, the workshop participants eager to return, the manuscript my publisher is preparing for production, and most importantly, the man before me and the girl across the room.

"It feels right," I answer. "Like I've finally found the story I'm meant to be living."

* * *

The compromise with Vera works better than I expected. Weekend events leave me tired but fulfilled, and I return to Harbour Point with stories to share and a deeper appreciation for the quiet life we're building. The writing workshop grows, attracting more participants each week until we have to create a waiting list.

One Wednesday evening in November, after our fourth successful workshop, I find Oliver in our bedroom, folding laundry with the methodical precision I've come to love.

"I got an email from the Young Writers of America competition," I tell him, leaning against the door frame.

His hands still on a half-folded shirt. "About Lily's story?"

"She's a finalist."

The shirt drops as Oliver's face lights up. "Are you serious?"

"Completely. They'll announce the winners next month in Boston."

"We have to tell her!"

"Tell me what?" Lily appears behind me, headphones around her neck.

Oliver and I exchange glances before I step toward her. "Your story, 'The Memory of Stars.' It's been selected as a finalist in the Young Writers competition."

Her eyes widen, mouth forming a perfect O. "But... that's impossible. There must be thousands of entries."

"And yours stood out," I tell her. "Just like I said it would."

She launches herself at me, arms wrapping tight around my waist. "Thank you for helping me. For making me believe I could do it."

Over her head, I meet Oliver's gaze, his eyes shining with emotion. This moment—this perfect, ordinary moment of family joy—is worth every compromise, every weekend away, every adjustment we've made.

"The ceremony is in Boston next month," I tell her as she pulls back.

"We'll all go together."

"Really? You'll be there?"

"Wild horses couldn't keep me away." I tuck a strand of hair behind her ear. "I already checked with Vera. No events that weekend."

Later, after Lily has called everyone she knows with her news, Oliver and I stand on the back porch, watching stars emerge over the water.

"You know what this means, don't you?" he asks, his shoulder warm against mine.

"What's that?"

"You're going to have competition. Another writer in the family."

Family. There's that word again, settling into my bones like it's always belonged there.

"I welcome it," I say, pulling him closer. "Some stories are better when they're shared."

Author's Note

Hi there,

Thanks for reading *Second Chapter*! I hope you enjoyed reading it as much as I did writing it. If you truly enjoyed it, please feel free to leave an honest review on the site of your choice. Reader reviews greatly influence the reading decisions of others, and help independent authors like myself stand out from the crowd!

You can also sign up for my newsletter at www.cgmacington.ca to receive a free copy of my novella *Ex Marks the Spot*!

Until next time,

C.G.

Also by C.G. Macington

Defying the Crown

When damaged hearts collide, can love overcome secrets?

Daniel isn't looking for love. After a devastating betrayal left him wary of relationships, he's focused on healing and rebuilding his life in New York City. But fate has other plans when a charming Danish stranger named Harald slides into his DMs.

Harald carries the weight of a crown he's not sure he can bear. As Denmark's heir apparent, he's trapped between duty and desire, forced to hide his true self behind palace walls. When he connects with Daniel online, he sees a chance at real happiness—if only he can keep his royal identity secret.

As their whirlwind romance spans from Manhattan's bustling streets to Copenhagen's historic charm, their connection deepens into something neither expected. But with Harald's throne-sized secret threatening to tear them apart, and Daniel's trust hanging by a thread, can their love survive the truth?

Emergency Contact

One look. One touch. One destiny.

The moment ER doctor Liam Winters locks eyes with paramedic supervisor Noah Bennet across a trauma room, something extraordinary happens. It's not just attraction—it's recognition, as if their souls have found each other again after lifetimes of searching.

Their connection is immediate and overwhelming, their bodies and minds in perfect sync both in and out of the hospital. When passion ignites between them, it's as undeniable as it is intense.

But when a prestigious fellowship threatens to separate them by a thousand miles, Liam must choose between the career he's always wanted and the love he never saw coming. In a heartbeat, he'll discover if some connections are truly meant to last forever.

Elemental: Forgotten Heritage

18-year-old orphan Noah lives a simple life in poverty with his grandmother. This changes overnight, as he comes into an elemental inheritance with god-imbued powers and learns he is the last descendant of an ancient line of royal magic. Noah is swept into a journey fleeing from a corrupted ruler hellbent on destroying the last remnants of Noah's lineage. His journey is filled with magic, danger, and a forbidden love with a man from his dreams. Now Noah's choices will save - or destroy - the Kingdom and those he loves.

www.ingramcontent.com/pod-product-compliance
Lightning Source LLC
Chambersburg PA
CBHW010435170726
48283CB00011B/3225